JEFFERY
GRIFFIN BROTHERS BOOK 4

KATHI S. BARTON

This is a work of fiction. Names, characters, places, and incidents are products of the author's imagination or are used fictitiously and are not to be construed as real. Any resemblance to actual events, locations, organizations, or persons, living or dead, is entirely coincidental.

World Castle Publishing, LLC
Pensacola, Florida
Copyright © 2023 Kathi S. Barton
Paperback ISBN: 9798891260283
eBook ISBN: 9798891260290
First Edition World Castle Publishing, LLC, August 7, 2023
http://www.worldcastlepublishing.com
Licensing Notes
Cover: Karen Fuller
Editor: Karen Fuller

Prologue

Charles, Charlie to most people who knew him, was so lost that he hadn't any idea if he was walking on the ground or the sky. He knew the difference, of course, but it was so dark out tonight that if there had been a moon shining, he couldn't see it. When he sat himself down on a log to get his bearings again, he paused in his thinking to look at what could have made the sound he'd heard.

Terrified out of his mind when he saw glowing eyes looking at him, Charlie sat as still as he could. The eyes grew larger and incredibly more shiny as the beast made his way to him. He didn't run, knowing that even if he knew where he was at the moment, the wolf would know it better. It would chase him down and kill him without any hesitation.

The wolf, a big gray fella, just stood there within a few inches of his outstretched legs. When he laid down, putting his heavy head onto his leg, Charlie had another moment of fear. The thing never took his eyes off him either. As soon as he felt he was brave enough to try and talk to the wolf, he was gone and in his place was a man.

A fully clothed man with the gray of the wolf's fur colored into his hair. Even his eyes were the same as the wolf, Charlie thought. Still, neither of them moved until the man sat back on his butt and regarded him.

"You live on the property not far from here. Is that correct?" Charlie told him he was only squatting there until they found him. But he was a mite lost. "Yes, I've been following you for some time. And in all that time, did you harm any other animal you came across, and there were plenty too. Why is that?"

"You mean the rabbit and the family of deer?" The man nodded. "I don't have a need for meat just now. I only kill when I have to. When my belly feels like it can't go another minute without some meat in it. And even then, I use it up to the best I can. What I can't use, I find some other animal that will use the rest. Why do you ask?"

"I'll get to that. You didn't seem that surprised when I changed from wolf to man. Can you tell me why that is?" He nodded and told him what he'd been seeing a lot of lately. "Yes, war will make a man wish for better times. So you were surprised but just wrote it off as being another strange thing that had no explanation. That's a very good reason, I think."

"They say that the war is about over. I don't know much about that. I can still hear shooting when I'm out and about. I don't have any land left because the soldiers took it all when they were coming through. Not that it was much more than a bunch of rocks and stumps, to begin with." The man only nodded. "I'm Charles Griffin. Most call me Charlie. A great deal more, but I ignore them. Not everybody was able to go to school all the time. I had my family to feed when my daddy up and got sick. Momma died a few weeks ago, and I've been roaming around since looking for work. I don't suppose you know anyone that might be wanting an extra hand around or two, do you?"

"I do, as a matter of fact. My name is Romeo Hank. The Hank is for when I need a last name. But I do have something that I'd like to propose to you, if you've the time to listen." Charlie told him he didn't have anything but time right now. "All right. "I have a medium-sized pack. You can see a few of them over there watching over us. They're all just wolves. I'm the only wolf shifter that I know. They're a good bunch. Hungry most of the time, but then all of us are, correct?"

"Yes. Some more than others. At least I can find me a bit of string and fashion me up a hook to use." Romeo told him that was excellent. "You need me to fish some fish out for you and your pack? I don't mind at all doing that for you. In fact, I'd be powerful happy to help you out."

"Not just yet. But I think that I will take you up on it soon. I have a daughter. Her name is Luna. Such a beautiful name, don't you think?" Charlie asked if it meant moon. "It does. Thank you. You're very well educated for a man with no means of living."

"My mom was a school teacher when I was born. They fired her, of course, when she had me. She didn't know my daddy, so that didn't help her none. She taught me to read and to figure. I can write too, but I do have to think about the spelling of things. Can you write?" Romeo said that he'd been given a great gift in that. "I think so too. When I find me a newspaper or some little old book, I treasure it for a bit. Then I pass it on if I can. I don't have to know the people in the paper. I just like reading about their stories. Are you going to tell me what this is about?"

"I am. I was working up to it, but I believe you to be a man that can be trusted with things in life. I would like to change you into a wolf. One such as I am. You'll be a man when you wish. A wolf when necessary. There will be magic as well as wealth." Charlie told him he didn't have a use for wealth, but food all the time would be nice. "That is precisely what I'm speaking about, Charlie, my good man."

Throughout the rest of the night and well into the morning, they spoke of things Romeo needed from him. It wasn't brought up again about him being changed, but Romeo did tell him that his daughter, and he found out that he, plain old Charlie was her mate. The soul reason that he'd not been harmed while wandering around in the woods.

"Do you understand what it is I want you to do?" Charlie said that he thought so. "No. I'm sorry. I can't allow you to go into this, only thinking you understand. Please, ask me anything that you'd like. You must be clear on this. I need for you to be clear on how it is I wish for you to someday take over for me."

Romeo never got upset with him when he asked his questions. If Charlie was honest with himself, which he usually tried not to be, he was afraid that Romeo had picked the wrong man. That he'd be better off finding himself someone else to take over his empire.

"You're the right man, Charlie. When I told you I'd been following you around, I want you to know that it wasn't just last evening. But for some time now. I've seen you share your last bit of food with people. Work for someone that cannot do for themselves and not take anything but a bit of bread and water. You're a very good man. A better man that I am." Charlie started to protest. "No. I'm correct in picking you as my replacement. And if that is some of your worry, being an Alpha, you've no worries there either. I will not leave this earth for the next until you are comfortable with what is needed of you. Now. If you've no more questions, I shall leave you to allow you to think about it. I'll be back here tomorrow so that you can tell me your answer. I know I have picked the right man, Charlie. It's something that you can do easily to save this pack and my daughter."

Luna followed him as he walked around. He'd thought about calling back Romeo and asking more questions, but he didn't. Sitting down again, his leg bothering him from sitting so long, he looked at the big, beautiful wolf.

"You're not really his daughter, are you?" She shook her head. "I didn't think so. Is there any more of the others that he claims are his children?" She nodded this time, and he determined by asking questions that it was one other female. "I don't know what to think about all this, to be honest with you. Are you my mate? Is he telling me the truth? I just don't know what to think."

She nodded or shook her head after each of the questions he put to her. Yes, she was his mate. Yes, Romeo was telling the truth. There were many more questions and answers. He was headed back to the area where he'd first seen Romeo when he felt the pain take his breath away as it slammed into his left shoulder.

Falling back, he hit his head and lay there while trying his best to catch his breath. That was when he heard the other gun shots, the wolf howling and trying to hide. Pulling Luna toward him, he whispered harshly into her ear, hoping that at least she'd understand him enough to know that she must warn the others.

"Go. Tell Romeo to hide the pack. To make sure you and your sister are safe." She didn't want to leave him, whimpering at him as she laid her head on his shoulder. "Go. Please. Run and escape before they hurt you too."

When she left him, Charlie closed his eyes. Opening them when he felt the shadow darken over him, he looked up in time to see the barrel of a large rifle. He was a goner. He knew that. He could only hope that Luna and the others were safe.

Chapter 1

Garfield was still sitting at his desk doing nothing but thinking about Drew, Allen Dresher's stepson and the two newest members of the pack. While Drew, ten, was a wolf, Allen wasn't. But it didn't seem to make any difference to either one of them that they were different.

Everyone had been so shocked at Drew's killing of Rocky, the pack leader to the pack that they'd been a part of, that even Edwin had been at a loss for words. According to Storm, Drew wasn't going to face any charges for killing a pack member, as Rocky had been sentenced to death beforehand for killing the mother of the little boy. It still amazed him that a ten-year-old boy had killed someone so quickly and seemingly without any nightmares about doing it.

Just two slashes to his throat with his clawed hand, and the man was gone. Good for everyone around, yes, but it still was slightly scary to him.

Getting up when the doorbell rang, Garfield welcomed Allen into his house. Sable, Garfield's mate and the love of his life had left an hour ago, and he wasn't expecting her back for another hour or two. Mom was helping her with the ins and out of them having a child, and he wanted her to remember everything she told her so that she could tell him.

Inviting Allen into the kitchen to have a drink with him, Garfield was hoping that he wasn't here for questions about Drew. He didn't have any answers. Edwin didn't even have them. The kid was going down in history as the bravest man-child he knew, that was for sure.

"I need your help with some money." Garfield told him he'd do whatever he needed for him. "Thank you. As you may or may not know, because Rocky killed Isabella, Drew's mother, Drew and I were given a great deal of money. Also, I was finally able to claim the insurance policy that she'd taken out on herself when her first husband had died. I was the beneficiary on that one. But I want Drew to have it. He'll need it more than I will, and I thought that coming from his mom, he'd take care to spend it wisely."

"You want me to invest it for the two of you?" Allen said that he didn't want Drew to have to work while going to college, and the young man did want to go to college. He wanted him to get a good education with the money. "All right. But you are aware that you're a part of our family as much as I am, correct? Drew is already calling my brothers uncle and their wives aunt. Even my parents are being called grandparents by him. We all love the two of you very much."

"Yes, I'm aware of that. It was all his doing, but I think it's best for him and me too." Garfield asked him if anyone had talked to him about being a part of the Griffin family and what that would mean for him and Drew. "I mean, they welcomed me into the pack and said that we're family too. But I don't know what you mean about anything else. If that's all that we get from you guys, then I couldn't be happier with it. It's lovely being a part of something with people that are especially nice. I love you guys as well."

"To begin with, you're an immortal." He shook his head. "Yes, you are. You and Drew both are. Drew will stop aging when he hits about twenty-five then he'll just be like us. You won't age at all from now on, nor will you put on any more weight than you have on your frame right now. You'll also be forever healthy."

"I don't understand. Like you?" He told him that he was an ancient. "I'm sorry. Perhaps I'm being dense. What do you mean by that?"

"My dad was alive during a time when the state wasn't even called Ohio. He lived through wars when they began in the seventeen hundreds. By then, my dad and my mom both were thousands of years old. Myself and my brothers were born to them during the beginning of their life together, so we're called ancients like my parents. All of us are old and have seen things that would boggle your mind." Allen said that wasn't possible. "It is, and it's the truth. I can't lie to you, Allen. Not that I would, but I'm telling you the truth." Allen got up to pace, and Garfield let him. It was a great deal to deal with, and he didn't blame him at all.

"I'm not saying that you're lying to me, but how is that even remotely possible? I mean, not to dismiss your claims of…do you have any idea how young you look?" Garfield laughed. "This isn't funny. You're older than dirt, my boy."

"Yes, well, I suppose you might be right on that. But I wanted to tell you that so that you'd understand that with age comes magic. And as you know, Storm and her sister, along with Jana and Sable, my mate, brought a great deal of magic to us as well. We're powerful, Allen, and so are you now." He asked him if that had anything to do with him being able to change his clothing with a thought. "Yes. I bet that scared you a bit. I know it did me when I realized I could do it."

"I was in a dressing room when it happened. I thought that I'd like the blue shirt better than the gray one that I was trying on, then I was suddenly wearing it. I asked Drew about it, and he acted like it was something he'd bene doing since birth." They both laughed. "I'm sorry. I'm sure you were making a point about telling me this, but my mind is still on the fact that we're immortal."

"Yes, I did have a point, but I understand. You won't ever die, Allen, nor will Drew. You won't have to worry about being sick, having cancer or anything else that might take you from us. We've been around for a long time, so we have a great deal of money too. And so long as we have money, you'll have it too." He said that they needed a house. "Oh, shit.

I forgot." Garfield rummaged around his desk and then handed over the envelope that had Allen's name on it. "Here is the deed to the house you were living in when we found you. It's bought and paid for. The furniture that was left behind by the previous owners you can keep or discard. That will be totally up to you and Drew. Also, there are accounts opened for you two all over town that both you and Drew can use as you need it. The pharmacy, grocery store as well as the hardware store too. If you do want to get rid of any of the things in the house, we ask that you donate them to a charity of your choice."

"This is too much." Garfield said that it was what family did for one another. Allen looked over the paperwork. "It says that there is a car and truck in the garage. Also a staff. I don't think we need all that."

"You'll be surprised at how handy a cook will be for you when Drew starts to fill out his wolf. It's an endless job of feeding him. Trust me, I know. The staff will help you too in keeping you both fed and safe. While you can't die, you can be kidnapped. We don't want that to happen either." Allen said that he didn't either. "Then you'll keep the staff around?"

"Yes. I'd be more afraid for Drew than for

myself, in that matter." Garfield didn't point out that Drew was a wolf and, therefore, better at slipping away, but Allen was speaking again. "I need to find a job. If for no other reason than to keep me busy. I've worked all my life, and just because we've had a windfall, I don't want to sit around idle. I think that would make me a bit more nutty than I already am." They both laughed.

"There are plenty of jobs within the family that you can take over for us at any time. What is it that you specialize in? Not that it matters. If you find something that you enjoy, we can get you trained on that too." Thanking him, Garfield watched as Allen paced. He noticed that it was something that he needed to do before he spoke. So that he could get all his thoughts in order. "I have a sister that I'd like to bring here sometime. Soon if you'd not mind. I've had her staying away before so she'd not get hurt if or when Rocky found us. I think that he would have used her — he more than likely would have used her to get to us. And her daughters. Even before Isabella was murdered, I was fearful of her coming around. Like I said, she has children."

"You bring her around, Allen and we'll make sure she has everything she needs as well. If she's your family, she's also ours." Allen said she had three daughters, triplets that she was raising on her own. "That's terrible for her, but when she gets here, there is plenty of family around to help her out with them. How old are they?"

"They're six years old. Blond hair, blue eyes. Just the cutest little girls you've ever seen. And real sweethearts too. She's never been married, however. If that makes a difference to you guys. The guy who fathered them was married, and Paige didn't know. Once she told him about the baby, she hadn't been aware of them being triplets by then. He told her that she needed to get rid of them because he didn't want his wife to know. As you can imagine, that didn't go over very well for her." Garfield laughed with Allen again. "I want to bring her here so she can finally have a permanent roof over her head. Food that doesn't come from a can, and the girls have more than just one dress a year to wear when they go out. She's forever barely making ends meet. I want the best for them as much as I do for Drew."

"Drew wants you to adopt him. Did you know that?" He said that they'd been talking about it. "Good. When you make a decision, let Storm know, and she'll put the paperwork in for you. It will be a done deal then." He thanked him again, but Allen seemed distracted. "Anything else I need to help you with? I'm here for you, Allen. You just say the word, and I'll do my best to get it for you."

"Can you go with me to get her? I have this strange feeling that I need to go soon to bring her here. Not even the thought of going tomorrow is making me feel better." Garfield stood up, telling him to always act on those feelings. "We're going right now?"

"Yes. Now. I only need to let Sable know, and we'll be going." They were on the road in ten minutes. Paige only lived in Cincinnati, but it was an eight-hour drive there and back. Since they were bringing four people back with them and who knew what else, Garfield rented them a cargo van with extra seating to drive so that they could be comfortable with them all riding together. By the time they reached Middletown, he knew as much about Paige as he did any other member of the family.

The drive was uneventful and boring. Drew, at the last minute, decided to go with them, and it was good for him to be helping out too. The little girls would be his cousins, as well as Paige being his aunt. Stopping to get some burgers when they reached

Jeffersonville. Trading driving with Allen, Garfield was happy to sit on the other side of the car for a while.

It was nearly dinner time when they pulled into the street that Paige lived on. The longer they drove down the street toward her home, the worse the houses got. They were barely what he'd call livable at the beginning. Now that he was looking at the ones that Allen's sister might live in, he was worried for their lives. And they were immortal. He was afraid when they pulled up in front of a sorry excuse for a duplex that looked like it should have been torn down with the other places around it decades ago. Getting out, Garfield kept an eye on their surroundings as Allen went to the door and knocked.

"Oh, dear god." Forgetting his fear for the sound of Allen's voice, Garfield took off toward the house after telling Drew to stay in the car. As soon as he was only a few feet from the door where Allen was standing, he could smell the blood. "Help me, Garfield. I think she's been hurt badly."

Calling an ambulance was a priority. Even as the police pulled up in front of the house, he could see people coming out of their homes to see what was going on. The ambulance arrived ten minutes after the police had and that had been a long time in coming too. Garfield was pissed off when one of the medics told him that they don't usually come out this time of night to this area. It's too dangerous.

"So what do you do, leave them to die out here because you don't take your job seriously enough to care?" The man told him to back off, or he'd be in the next ambulance. "I'd like to see you try that. Come on. Show me what you have."

"Uncle Garfield." Stretching his neck, hearing it pop, he told Drew he was sorry. "It's all right to me, but you're scaring the girls."

By the time Paige and one of her daughters were being taken away after giving what money he had on him to take them to the hospital, Garfield had the other two finding things that they wanted to take with them. There was no way he was going to allow them to come back here. He was glad when he saw the packed bags for the family next to the front door. And was glad that Allen had called his sister when they started out to tell her to get ready.

It didn't take them long to get loaded up. Basically, because there was very little that was worth taking. And even that was questionable. The house, despite it being such a dump on the outside, looked very nice on the inside. It was clean though very worn out. The fridge didn't work, the children told them, so there was a cooler with ice on the floor with milk and eggs in it. There was very little else in the house to speak of in the way of food. He wondered why they were living like this, then decided to ask.

"Do you know what happened?" Allen said he'd tell him later. He then reminded him about their link. Allen said he was too pissed off to talk right now and just looked out the window. Reaching for Storm, he told her what was going on as well as what they encountered when they arrived.

Give me a moment here. I'm hacking into the police station now. I'll also take care to find out about the medics telling you that. I have a feeling that things are going to get worse before — here is it. The call came in two hours ago. Two fucking hours and they only just arrived when you got there? Heads are going to be lopped off. You can bet on that. Anyway, it says here that a child called in that her mother had been shot and that she needed someone to come to the house. There were noises in the background that the 911 operator noted in his notes. Screams, as well as a loud male voice. Two shots were fired while he was on the line with the child, and he hung up on her. When she called back, she got a different operator who told her not to call in again. *I'm telling you right now, Garfield, I'm going to take Rain with me, and we're going to fucking clean house down there.*

Just tell me what you found, honey, so I can take care that none of the others are hurt. She said she didn't like to be calm about what happened. *I'm not, either. But we really need to get this taken care of in an order.*

One of the little girls said it was the landlord that hurt her mother and sister. She said that mom had been trying to keep up with the rent, but he kept changing the price to go up each week, and her mom was trying to make ends meet." She read the notes on the incident and then told Garfield what she'd been able to find in the archives.

So she's been having issues with her landlord for some time, and without the police coming around when she calls, he thinks that he can get away with whatever he wants. Please tell me that you're going to find him for me. She told him that she was going to find him for her. *Just be careful that you don't leave enough evidence around that you get caught.*

Did you just tell me that I can go ahead and kill this prick so long as I'm careful? I think I love you more than Edwin right now. He smiled, knowing that his brother wouldn't find that to be funny in the least bit. *Rain and I are going to come there now. You just take care that the little family is all right. Bring them here if you can tonight, and we'll make sure that they have a better life.*

That's what Allen and I were talking about when he asked me to come with him today. His sister has had a rough life, it seems. Well, we're in front of the hospital now. I'll let you know what I know here in a little while. He entered the mostly full emergence department and had to ask three times as to where Paige and her daughter were. *I need you to do something for me, Storm. They're not going to operate on either of them because they don't have insurance, even though it's life or death for the mother. I know that's against the law, but I think that as long as they treat the wounds, that's all they have to do. Can you get some asses rolling so that they can be fixed up enough for me to bring them home so that they can get proper care?*

He knew that he sounded pissed off. He was. He was about as pissed as he'd ever been in his life. When the phone rang next to the desk he was standing by, Garfield knew the moment that someone was getting their ass reamed by Storm. After she hung up, the nurse ran around telling people to get their asses in gear and help the Dresher family. He was going to have to get Storm a big gift for helping him in this.

Removing the bullet wasn't a long surgery. However, once they got her into surgery and took some X-rays, they found broken ribs. Another bullet hole in her back as well as enough cuts and scratches on her body that totaled about two hundred stitches. The little girl, Amy, didn't fare much better than her mother, but she was young, and her body was able to bounce back better. He personally thought that Paige had been skipping meals for her daughter to have enough to eat. It was what he knew any of the women in his family as well as his entire family, would have done in the same circumstances.

Paige also had broken ribs on both sides of her body. A busted lip that required stitches both inside and outside her mouth. And trauma to the back of her head. Had she laid there over night with the wound to her head, the medics had said they'd not have come, the surgeon told him that she would have died. As it was, Garfield gave them both a bit of his blood to help them along to being well enough to take home.

Taking the other two little girls to a hotel, knowing that they'd be in the hospital over night, they ordered pizza for them all and watched some television. Allen kept the girls eating, and as soon as he put them to bed after them playing in the tub, they were asleep. Stress could do that, he knew first hand. Even Drew was asleep in no time.

"She's going to be all right, you think?" Garfield told him that he'd give her more of his magic if she didn't look good in the morning. "Thank you for that. I was talking to Libby, and she said that Mr. Hopewell comes by once a month trying to get into her mom's pants. I'm not sure she understands what that means, but she knows enough to hate the man on site."

They talked about getting them home and what was going to happen when they got there. He heard from Rain once and Storm twice. Mr. Hopewell wasn't going to be a problem anymore, and he would never be found. He didn't ask though he wanted to know what they'd done. He was just happy that it had been taken care of. To him, having a quick death was more than the man deserved.

Garfield didn't rest much. He was thinking about the way some men, and he knew women could treat the opposite sex. His parents would have skinned him alive, literally, if he'd tried anything like what he'd witnessed tonight. Or, for that matter, over the past few weeks, he'd been seeing with other couples. He was going to make it a point to keep an eye out for happenings like this one from now on.

I've sent the plane to bring you all home. Paige is going to need to be in a place where she can lie down rather than being in a van for hours. Also, there will be a doctor on board that will monitor her and Amy while they're coming here. He thanked Storm. *No worries about that. I've also hired a nurse to go to Allen's home so that she'll get the best of care there as well. Also, I've made sure that the girls have their rooms set up. I cheated in looking into what they wanted, so it'll be something that they can have while getting rested up.*

"I can't thank you enough for this." She said that it had been her pleasure. She was looking forward to meeting Paige and her daughters. *"The girls are wonderful. Even though they've been through hell in the last few nights, they're having fun with Drew. He's been a good cousin to them."*

"Of course he is. He's a great kid." He thanked her again as he got dressed. The girls had all taken a shower this morning before him, and he was happy that he'd remembered to get extra towels for them to all use. They were headed to the hospital when Sable contacted him.

"You should see this house. It looks like a pink rocket exploded in the bedrooms." They laughed. "I've gotten them some things like computers to use. I know that we might be doing too much, but I find that I don't care. I want them to have some fun while their mom is recovering."

"They had so little when I picked them up. Everything that the girls had was in a single large trash bag. Their mothers wasn't much at all in that her things fit into a small box. I hurt for them." She said that she did too. "All right, love. I'm going to see about feeding these little ones something bad for them and head over to the hospital. Hopefully, we'll be able to leave here sometime today. I hope so. I miss you."

"I miss you too. I love you so much." He told her that he loved her as well, and they closed the connection.

Paige was awake when they arrived, but he could almost taste her pain. She was refusing the meds in order to see her children and to make sure that they were all right. As soon as she was assured that they were all fine, he insisted that she take something for it. She didn't argue with him but nodded. Calling in the nurse, Paige was drifting off almost as soon as the needle left the IV port.

Taking the kids to get some lunch, Garfield was enjoying himself. They were great kids, all three of them, and he was happy that they seemed to be bouncing back better than he was. Even Allen was able to have some fun with the girls.

It was three days later that they were able to leave the area, but it was time well spent in the area. There had been a big shake-up at not only the police station but also the hospital. By the time they left, more than half of the administrative team had been fired, and all of the police department had been replaced with FBI agents that were called in to see into the allegations of theft, murder and a lot of other things that he was just hearing about. He'd never been so happy to be a part of something as he was this week. Heads were rolling, yes, but there would be a much better outcome for a lot of people needing the services of the places that had been taken care of.

The flight home was short and uneventful. Libby was feeling better than her mom and was able to sit with her sisters. Their bond was tight, and he was glad to see that they also took care that their mother was getting the best of care. Each of them took turns checking on Paige to make sure of it.

Once Paige and her daughters were settled into their home they were sharing with Allen, Garfield was finally able to feel better. He'd been so stressed out while down there that he'd never been so happy to be home in his life. Since he was so exhausted from it all, he and Sable laid down to nap. Snuggling up with her in their bed was the best thing that had happened all week. When he woke, not only was he alone, but there wasn't anyone in the house either. Getting up, he reached out to Sable to figure out where she had gone.

I've been working on a project since you were gone. A hotline that abused people can call that will get them safely out of their situation. I didn't come up with the idea, but this bunch of college men that put it out there that they'd be there for them if they called. Even going as far as moving them out of the place they were in to get them to a better place. He told her that was brilliant. *I thought so too. Anyway, it's going to be a way that they can safely call into the hotline without the abuser knowing what is going on. I've not worked out the details on that as yet, but I'll get there.*

I have all the faith in the world that you will. I was thinking that this might be something that my mom would like to help you on. She's been an advocate for helping the abused for a while now. You don't have to let her help you, but I'm sure she'd enjoy it. Sable told him that she was here with her now, helping with the details of it all. *Great. Did you ask her about us having our baby? I'm sure she has lots of information for us.*

Not only did she, but she said that I should take your crib home with us the next time we're over. She said she has boxes of clothing that she knitted over the years that she is going to divide up for all of the boys she calls you guys. He said he thought that dad had made the beds for them all. *He did. And the rocking chairs that we're to take as well. When Charlie was making the first one for Edwin, he decided that he was going to make one for each of his children so that they could rock their own babies in the future. I think that's the sweetest thought ever. We'll be able to get it with the bed sometime.*

Garfield loved his parents so much. The fact that they had thought ahead by making it so that they would have a piece of their childhood when they had children made him think that they were the best parents ever. He hoped that he could be half the father that his dad had been, and he'd count himself lucky.

After having some early lunch, Garfield made his way to Allen's home. He was only there to make sure that they didn't need anything but hung around so that Allen could run to the store to get some much-needed supplies for his nieces. He thought that even with them only being six, they were very organized about nearly everything.

"What sort of much-needed supplies do six-year-olds need?" Allen told him what they were doing and then showed him the list they'd given him. "So they want to make their mom a card, and you need to get them...does this say fancy hearts? I'm not sure what that is, but you'd better not mess it up."

Amy, feeling much better, sat down next to him and explained. "We want the kind of hearts that look like paper cut outs. All fancy and stuff. I had one once, but it got blood on it when I lost a tooth on account of Mr. Hopewell knocking it out when he came to see our mom. Oh, and we'd like some of those scissors that cut wavy lines and stuff too." She was adding to the list even as Allen was gathering up his wallet and car keys. It amazed him that the three of them could be so cavalier about their treatment when living in the other house. He supposed it was because they were children. "He's going to mess this up, huh?"

"Maybe, but you'll cut him some slack, right? I mean, it's been a long time since he's been around such beautiful little girls." She rolled her eyes at him. When Libby joined them at the table, she sat on his lap rather than taking the chair. He asked her if she thought he was a chair.

"No. But I know that you won't hurt me when I'm close to you. I like that." He told her how sorry he was that she'd been treated like she'd been. "I'm not happy that it happened, but we'll all still together and breathing. That's what mom says all the time when the landlord would come over. Also, she said that what doesn't kill us makes us stronger. I think that's a bunch of bull crapola. Mom was beaten up all the time, and it didn't make her any stronger to fight back. Men are pigs."

"Not all of them are, honey. I'm not. Nor are my brothers." She eyed him, asking him how many brothers he had. "Five. All of us are big men, but we'd never hurt a woman. They're excited to get to meet you guys too."

"You should tell them to bring over some food, and we can have a cook out. We've never had one before." He asked her why not before he thought about it. "The landlord wouldn't allow us to have anything out on a grill. Mom tried to cook them in the stove once. The top of the oven got really red hot. But the stove broke, and we only had half-cooked hot dogs. Have you ever had macaroni salad? I've not. You should add that to the list, too, for us to have. Like a celebration that we're set free from all that crap."

The three of them were talking about all the things that went with a picnic when Glory came to join them. Of the three of them, Glory was the most shy. But when she had something to say, she wouldn't hesitate. Nor when she thought you were in the wrong. He'd noticed, too, that they were all forgiven of small transgressions. He figured that their mother had taught them that too. She was a good mom, Garfield decided.

"I love chips. The kind that has sour cream on them. I had them once when I was really little, and I have been craving them since." He didn't know how little she could have possibly been because she was only six, but he told her that was his mom's favorite too. "You don't like them?"

"I'm not a huge fan of chips at all, really. I know that my wife doesn't care for them either. Now French fries? I could eat a vat of them." They giggled and began talking about going to school soon and what they would do when it snowed. "We'll have to get you some winter stuff so we can go sledding. Mom and dad have a long hill behind their house that is the most fun of winter when it's covered in snow."

By the time Allen returned, he'd bet that he knew more about the girls than their own mother did. He knew what they liked and didn't like in the way of food. The kind of clothing they preferred when it was hot out. He told them that he and Sable had a large pool they could use, and that excited them to no end. They were family, and he couldn't have been happier about having them around than he was about Drew and Allen.

He also found out more about their living conditions prior to them going to get them. He also knew that their father didn't pay child support because he didn't believe they were his daughters. Garfield also understood something else about the three of them, they would scream at each other when they had a point to be made, but they'd kill someone if they tried to hurt one of the others. He thought that was the same as he and his brothers.

Allen returned with six large shopping bags of

supplies. When he said he had more in the car, the girls followed him out. Garfield started emptying bags on the dining room table and separating out the items. Allen had found the fancy hearts, it seemed, and he got them in different sizes and colors. There were the wavy scissors, lots of glitter as well as glue and pipe cleaners to play with as well. He could almost taste the glitter as it made its way into every crack and crevasse of their new digs.

Garfield headed home before they started spreading the glitter around. There was no way he was going to be a sparkly wolf if he could help it. He knew that he'd never hear the end of it. Not that he wouldn't have enjoyed having fun with them. But he really did have some things that needed to be taken care of that he had left behind when he'd traveled to Cincinnati to get the little family.

His heart was lighter as he headed home. He was also in a better mood. If he thought that he could bottle up the girls' laughter and happiness, he'd never have to work another day in his life. It was like a good wine to him, to hear laughter with no thought to how loud or crazy you sounded.

Chapter 2

Paige didn't hurt as much as she had when they first got to Allen's home, but she was still sore. Especially her ribs. Her doctor had told her to get up and move around. It would help with the broken ribs but not to overdue it for the same reason. Glancing at the extra-large get-well card that the girls had made her had Paige smiling and holding back tears. It must have cost Allen a fortune to buy all the things for it, and she was so grateful for him doing that for her daughters. In the hallway, she encountered Drew. She loved this little boy as much as she did her own daughters.

"Want me to walk with you, Aunt Paige?" She said she'd like that, especially after yesterday's little fall. "I'm really glad that I had to come back to the house yesterday to get my hat. I don't want to think about you having to have lain there on the ground for so long. I'm so happy that you weren't hurt very much more."

"I am as well. Also that I didn't have to go back to the hospital. I'm tired of being there." They walked down the long hallway and were headed back the other way when her cell phone rang. "I still don't know why I need this sucker. Anything that Allen needed to tell me could have waited until he got home. It seems a waste of money."

"I have myself one too. I like knowing that no matter what, I can get in touch with someone. You should be too." She told him that she supposed so. "The girls don't have one; however, I think they're going to beg you for one for the each of them."

"They will have to wait, I'm afraid. I can't keep taking from Allen, or he'll be as broke as I am." Drew told her that they were family and that the Griffins had taken them in as well. "That doesn't mean that we have to drain them dry. I like the ones that I've met so far. But they are really big men, aren't they?"

"Yes. Big but gentle like a lamb, Grandma Griffin says. Until they need to protect one of the family. Then they're wolves on a mission." Paige had heard that they were all wolves from Allen. He told her, too, that they were ancients. She even, on some level, knew what that meant. That didn't mean that she believed it, but she did know what it was supposed to mean. "You're doing much better. Would you like to go downstairs now? I know that the girls are at grandma's house today. They're baking cookies to give away to the children at the school for the moms that don't bake."

"I love cookies." She did too. Not so much to eat but to have around when the holidays came around. Paige couldn't remember the last time that she'd had the funds to just bake a bunch of cookies for her girls. It hurt her how very little she'd been able to afford at all. "When is Allen coming home? Do you know?"

"At dinner time, he told me. But he said that if we needed him sooner, he could leave work early. He's working for the pack now." She stopped moving and asked him what he was talking about. "Uncle Edwin is the leader of the wolf pack that I'm in. You knew that I was a wolf, right?"

"I think someone mentioned it. I don't remember who now. Are you really a wolf?" He grinned and asked her if she wanted to see his wolf. "No. I mean, not yet. There has been a lot going on, and I'm — have the girls seen him? I mean, don't if they've not seen him. I don't want them afraid."

"They've seen him. And we play in the yard together. It's been fun for all of us. Especially Amy. She's still hurting in her heart about what happened to you." She looked out into the back yard, where she could see her daughters playing now. They must have returned from Mrs. Griffins early. They seemed to be adjusting to this new life much better than she was. "Aunt Paige, you're going to be all right. You know that, don't you?" She looked at him, wiping away the tears that kept coming at an alarming rate lately.

"You know where we came from, Drew. You know that we had less than homeless people do living in that place. I don't want them to get used to anything and have it snatched away from them." He sounded so sure when he told her that they'd not. "I know you believe that honey, but I've been in the real world a lot longer than you have, and I know how people can be when they are determined to make someone fail."

"You should understand that the Griffins are that determined to make sure that you and my cousins are safe too. The same as they've done for Allen and

I." He looked at the back yard as he continued. "I was ready to die when they found us. Allen was nearly dead as well. We'd been hiding out for so long that I was just too tired to go on. I'd been taking care of Allen since he'd been hurt, and my mom had been killed right in front of me. Rocky did that, the pack leader where we lived. I didn't trust anyone anymore, but I've come to trust that the Griffins are just what they say they are. Trustworthy people that only want to help. You'll notice that I didn't say what was best for us. They didn't say that because I was told that we're the only ones that know what is best for us. They're a good family, and I trust them with everything that I have."

She wanted to believe him. She needed to, as a matter of fact. But it was hard. She'd been going from the burner to the frying pan since she'd found out she was going to have a baby. It seemed to her that people would forever say one thing only to do something else. When Drew squeezed her hand, she looked where he was looking.

In the back yard with her girls was the biggest animal she'd ever seen. It was a wolf, she realized as she made her way frantically to the back doors. As soon as she opened the door and stepped out onto the porch, she was knocked on her ass by another big wolf. Struggling to get out from under it, she saw Drew coming toward her with the other wolf at his side. Screaming to get to her daughter, Drew sat down beside her head and smiled at her.

"I promise you, Aunt Paige, the girls are more than all right. This is Uncle Jeffery. Not Jeff, he said but Jeffery. He wants me to tell you what he's saying so that you'll get calm. I've already told him that I think it would take a lot more to get you to calm down, but he said he wanted to try." She said that her girls needed to get in the house. "That's where they're headed in a few minutes. The wolf that is with them will change once she gets into the house. That's Grandma, Uncle Jeffery's mom. Are you willing to listen to him? Well, me and him, I guess."

She looked up at the big wolf. Christ, she'd never seen a dog this close, much less a wolf. Paige had a feeling that not all wolves would be as big as this guy. Moving her hands slowly to his fur on his shoulder, she smacked him there. And all he did was throw back his head and howl. It was both wonderful and scary at the same time. She asked Drew what he was doing.

"Okay. I'm going to tell you, but I'm just the

messenger. All right?" She looked at the little boy and asked him what that was supposed to mean. "You've only been here a few days, Aunt Paige, but even I can tell that you're freaking out at every little thing that happens. No one is going to hurt you here. Ever. I promise you that. Now, Uncle Jeffery wants me to tell you that he'll shift and talk to you, but he's not sure if he has the ability to change into clothing once he shifts. We can all do it, but he said that he's never tried it—"

"Shift into clothing? Are you saying that if he were to shift into whatever he was before being a wolf that—" Drew assured her that Jeffery was a wolf and man, like the others. "All right, shift into a man that there will be a good possibility that he might be naked? Is that what he wants me to know?" Even to her own ears, she sounded frantic. She couldn't imagine what sort of impression she was making with her nephew and girls. Clearing her throat, she looked up at the man-wolf over her. "Tell him if he shifts right now, I'm going to hurt him in ways that he's never thought of."

"He can hear you, Aunt Paige. It's just you that can't hear him." There was a tone there, one that she didn't care for, but she, right now, was choosing to ignore it. "He said to tell you that he was walking through the forest when he felt your fear. He didn't know why he was able to feel it until he touched — is that what she is to you, Uncle Jeffery?"

The lick to her face startled her. The roughness of his tongue made her think that she'd been licked by a cat rather than a dog of sorts. When Drew laughed, she turned to look at what he was doing now that was so funny. However, he'd gone into the yard to be with her girls. Paige looked up at Jeffery again.

"You hurt anyone in my family, and I will — stop licking my face. That's gross. I don't know where your tongue has been." She moved her head to the side and glared at him. "You're not funny. I'm not sure that you are actually laughing, but if you are, I'm going to hurt you."

You shouldn't be able to hurt me. Looking around, she looked back at the wolf. *Yes, it's me. Since I licked you, we have a connection now. No one can ever hear us when we speak like this. However, now that you and I have connected, you can also speak to my brother Edwin. He's the alpha of our pack. Storm, too, should you need her.*

"I don't know who you think you are, but I don't want you talking to me in my head." He told her that he belonged to her. "What's that supposed to mean? I don't belong to anyone but those girls over there."

I belong to you. The girls too. I will lay down my life for the four of you, as will my family. She asked him what he was talking about. *I'm your mate, Paige. The two of us are mates.*

"I don't have any idea what that means. Other than what I've read in smut books." She eyed him carefully. "It also says that we're to have epic sex. I no more believe that than I do that my landlord is going to turn over all the money that I spent on trying to keep my daughters safe when we lived in Cincinnati."

I hope we will, but that will be entirely up to you when and if that happens. I'm going to roll off of you now. One of your little girls is upset because she can feel that you are. If you'd not mind telling them that I'd rather die than to harm you, I think that will reassure her. She asked him who was going to reassure her. *Anyone in my family can attest that I'm a good person. All of us are. And as for your landlord. He's dead.*

"I'm sorry, what?" He told her that Mr. Hopewell had been killed the night that he'd shot her. "By you? I should hope that if you did that, it's not going to get you into my pants any more than it did him."

Your daughters, they told my brother that he was trying to do that. I don't think they know what that means. She looked at her little girls, playing in the grass, more than likely the first real grass they'd seen since being born and watching the two of them. *Are you going to allow me to roll off you and you not run off?*

"I won't. Did they really tell someone that?" Jeffery moved to her side and shifted. His body was covered with clothing, for which she was grateful. He told her then that he could never lie to her. "Yeah? Pull the other leg. That one is long enough. Everyone lies. Especially men when they find something that they want and will get it at all costs."

"You're going to need to start believing in me at some point. I have plenty of time to wait. But no, I cannot lie to you. Nor will I ever leave you. For any reason. You are my heart now, and I cannot continue on with my life without you in it." She stared at him. "What is it you'd like to ask me that someone else might well lie to you about?"

"Anything?" He nodded. "All right. Why did you leap on me?" He told her. She looked to the woods were he had pointed to and asked him if he was sure. "I mean, this person could have just been out taking a walk or something. Not anything to do with me."

It's the girls' biological father. I know this because they smell slightly like him. Not in a bad way, but biologically they do." He said that to her through the link he'd formed. As he continued, Libby came to sit on her lap. *I've also read his mind and why he's around here. It's because of his wife. She has a child by Howard. However, she wants a daughter. He told his wife that you were to have his child a while back and that he'd make a big stink about you lying to him about the baby and taking it from you. Only if it's a girl. However, since he has no idea what you delivered, not even the sex of the baby, he didn't bother with the girls today because he thought they were the person that lives here. The children weren't yours, and you're babysitting them. Once he figures it out, I'm afraid that he'll come for them. His mind is full of things that you supposedly owe him. One of the girls is top of his list. Also, the fact that you told his wife that he was fucking you. His words, not mine. Did you really tell his wife?*

Yes. When he left me without a penny when I told him I was pregnant, I decided to end his affairs. Howard wants to prove that I'm unfit or something, I'm assuming. Something along those lines. Jeffery nodded, and she looked at the woods again. *I need to leave here then.*

Howard, Howard Murry is his name, and he has money to fight me for them. And I don't want to get Drew or Allen hurt because of him.

I can help you if you'd allow it. My family can and will if you want. Perhaps even if you didn't want their help. They're pushy and can be a bit scary. She asked him what they could do. *Plenty more than Howard can do, that's for sure. I work for the government, as does Storm and my brother Edwin is a highly decorated retired army. Also, Storm and Rain have a great deal of magic that they can use to see what it is that he has in the way of back up. Or, for that matter, any money that he might well have. And how he'd gotten it. Which I can guarantee you isn't nearly as much as you and I have now that we're mates. Also, and this is something that you and the girls need to know now, you're immortal. A true immortal in that you'll never be killed. All four of you are. The girls will stop aging by the time they're in their mid-twenties. Also, none of you will ever be sick again for any reason. Allen and Drew have the same magic.*

This is too much. He told her he was sorry. *I'm not being pissy, but this is just — I just realized that I don't hurt. Not at all.*

That's because I'm your mate. I belong to you. She told him that he kept saying that, that he was hers.

You are. I really do belong to you. Forever and beyond. I will, as I said, lay down my life for you.

A woman and a man appeared on the deck with them. Not walked up on it but just popped there. It was Libby that told her who they were. Storm and Edwin had come to welcome her to their family. Apparently, her daughters were already calling them aunt and uncle. She wished for just a moment that she'd never gotten out of bed today.

~*~

There was something different about Paige. While he couldn't put his finger on it right then, Howard knew that if he could see her closer, then he'd figure it out. She sure did look good enough to take on as a mistress again. Pacing the hotel room that he had rented to come here, Howard wondered how she'd ended up out of the apartment complex that he'd owned. And getting in touch with Hopewell was proving to be just as difficult. He didn't ever bother her, but he made sure that Hopewell knew that she wasn't to get any favors given to her. The man had never mentioned a kid living with her, now that he thought about it.

Howard looked at his cell phone before answering it. It was his wife, Rachel. She'd been calling him every two hours since he'd told her where he was going. And why. She wanted a daughter, and he told her that he'd find out if Paige had had one by him. Christ, if she'd just get off his back, he might well have been done by now. As soon as she hung up, no doubt leaving him a scalding message again, his cell rang again. This time it came up as the county seat in the town where Paige had been living.

"Mr. Murry?" He said that it was him. "I've found the records that you asked for. However, your name isn't on the certificates that you told me you were. It's just a blank space for the name of the father. I can't give you the information over the phone. You'll have to come here at the County seat and buy copies and find out for yourself what the sex of the babies are."

"I don't have time for that. I'm not even there anymore but near Paige. Just tell me the sex, and I'll send you a hundred bucks." The woman told him that it wasn't worth her losing her job then she hung up on him. "Mother fuck. All she had to do was tell me, and that would have been the end of it."

Howard thought that there was no way that he'd fathered a daughter. He was just too manly for him to have planted a girl in anyone. All the other women he'd fucked had had boys, and there was no reason for him to think that Paige was any different. He was potent, that was all. He didn't even know why he'd suggested to Rachel that she might have had him a daughter. There wasn't any way that she'd had a daughter. This was just taking up too much of his time right now. He could be home basking in all the things that he'd purchased with Rachel's money. Games and shit like that.

Lying down on the bed, he thought of all the things that his wife had told him about having any more affairs after she had found out about the last woman he'd fucked. Thanks to Paige telling her about them and what he'd done about her being pregnant. That had been the final straw, Rachel had told him. That if another woman came to her about him, she was going to bury him up to his neck in an ant hill. He didn't understand her logic on that, but then she was a female and didn't have much in the way of smarts like he did.

Since he'd had to sign a prenup when he married Rachel, he'd been told by her attorney that if he left her, he'd be in worse shape than he'd been before they wed. He didn't know how that could have been possible. He'd been living out of his car by then and nary a nickel to his name. Knocking her up had been the smartest and stupidest thing he'd ever done.

While it had been harder to have an affair after that, it certainly made it all the more thrilling to have them. All the sneaking around and playing the good husband had excited him to the point where he was having more affairs than he'd had before. Howard now had four women that he was fucking, and he'd never been caught.

"Women are just stupid." He'd thought that his entire life. Even his mom had been about the stupidest woman ever born. She'd have dinner on the table every night at six sharp, and Dad would come out of the living room while the big clock was still chiming, sit at the table, eat in silence, then go back to the living room. Howard couldn't remember a single conversation that they'd ever had at the dining room table. "Why? Why did she even care that he was fed?"

Dad had never beaten his mom. Not that he knew of anyway. Nor had he ever raised his voice to her. Again, not that he'd ever heard. Yet she did the same thing every single day so that his dad would have a meal when it was time. Mom also did all the laundry and even mowed the lawn for his father. She did it all for not even a kind word or even a show of affection between them. Back then, he thought that it had been just mean of his father. Now…well, not so much.

When he'd married Rachel, he'd decided that he was going to treat her better. While he hadn't any idea why that thought had been in his head, the day after they returned from the honeymoon, all thanks to her money, he'd fallen into the same pattern as his father had. Eating at a certain time. Barely paying any attention to Rachel, and when their son had come along, he'd had very little to do with him. Just as his father had done. Now Rachel was bitching about wanting a daughter.

That was the one thing that he'd never figured out about women. Why they thought that having a child that was female was going to make their world a little better. It wasn't as if she couldn't go out and buy whatever she wanted. Hell, she did that all the time. But having a girl was something that she'd been complaining about since she'd delivered Howie. She'd wanted him to father her a girl child.

However, he'd nipped that in the bud when he'd father about ten children in his little side fucking, and he decided that he didn't want anyone else calling him dad. So taking a little break from the wife, he'd gone off and had himself snipped. To him, it had been worth all the pain just knowing that there wouldn't be anyone else out there that he'd father. The ten or so that he had now was more than he wanted to think about.

Deciding that he was going to splurge on a big, nice dinner, he made his way to the front desk to ask them where he could go and get a good meal. Prime rib was all he could think of, and he was pleasantly surprised when he told him that they were serving that very thing in their dining room tonight. Once he was seated and ordered, all thoughts of Paige and her son were out of his thoughts. It was dinner time, and he was suddenly starved. Then a man sat across from him, taking his bread basket and handing it to the table next to him.

They were related, both the other table of men and the man sitting with him. Any fool with even terrible eyesight could tell that. Not only were they big as houses, but they had the same look about them. Men that not only got what they wanted but also didn't care who they stepped on to get it. A second bread basket was brought to him when he asked for it, and again, it was taken from him.

"What the fuck do you think you're doing?" He told him that they were hungry. "In the event, it might have slipped your vision, this is a restaurant. Order yourself something and get the hell away from me."

"You're to stop looking into trying anything with Paige and her family." He asked him what business it was of his what he did. "I'm going to marry her and adopt her children if she'll allow it. You being out there wanting one of what is hers is making me nervous. When I'm nervous, I tend to lash out at the person doing it."

"Children? She's only got the one. A son." The man shook his head and said that she had three little girls. Triplets. "Then what did she do with my son?" The pop to his forehead hurt, knocking his head back hard enough that he heard it pop.

"She didn't have a son. Paige had three of the most beautiful little girls I've ever seen. And they're going to be mine soon. Is there something wrong with you?" Howard told the man that that was impossible. That he only sired men. "Yet I just told you that it was impossible. She had triplets. Little girls that, thankfully, look just like her."

"I don't believe you." The man just shrugged. When his dinner was brought to him, the man handed that, too, to the table next to them. "What the fuck are you doing with my dinner? You're going to pay for my meal. I hope you know that."

"I'm not paying for shit for you, dumbass." Howard thought about standing up, just for a moment, when the two men at the other table stood. They were about a foot taller than him. Not that he was all that tall, but he knew when to stay seated and behave. He wasn't stupid by any means. "I'd have to disagree with that notation in your head. You're stupid if you think that Paige is going to let you anywhere near her daughter. Nor will I. So, if you want to live longer than the next month, I suggest that you leave her and her children alone."

"What if I were to pay you for one of them?" When he didn't answer him, Howard continued. "She'll still have two of them. My wife, she only wants a daughter. It'll even us up, me and Paige. She'll have her two daughters if what you say is true. And I'll have a son and a daughter. Seems only fair to me that she just hands one over. I'll even allow her to pick which one. Surely there is an ugly one or a stupid one in the lot. Well, stupidest. Just tell her that you have a buyer for one, and I'll meet you someplace where we can do the exchange. It can't be too much, you understand. I mean, she's had them all for what? Ten or so years?"

"Six. And you cannot be serious in thinking she'd just hand over one of her children, are you?" Howard asked him why he'd care what she did with them. They were his kids too. "They're not your kids, as a matter of fact. Your name is nowhere on their birth certificates. Not to mention, you've never paid a dime to have them raised either."

"Water under the bridge now, don't you think? I mean, like I said, she's had them this long. She can't expect me to pay her for support when she was making it before I came along." The man asked him if he'd known where Paige was all this time. And the troubles that she'd been having. "Sure. I own that building. Well, my wife does. It was a nice income for us and with very little return. Hey, I just thought of something. She's been paying me child support all along."

The man looked at the other two people at the other table and then back at him. Howard didn't know why, but he had a feeling that the man found him lacking in some way. Taking in a deep breath to make himself bigger, he let it out quickly when one of the men from the other table stood up again and smacked him upside the head. While he was trying to figure out what the hell he'd done for them to have done that to him, the man across from him told him to shut up and listen.

"You're going to leave Paige alone. And her daughters. If you so much as breathe around them, I'm going to rip your throat out and enjoy watching you bleed out." When he looked down at the table like he was, he could see the large fucking paw that was over his hand. As it dug deeply into his skin, Howard cried out. Then he took his paw to his mouth and licked the blood there. Howard felt his cock inch its way into his ass hole. Hiding from the monster sitting with them. "You can't fart now that I won't know about it. Every time you think of her, I'll know. And when you come near them again, ever, I'll know. Then I'll do just what I said. Rip your throat out. Do you understand me?"

Swallowing, Howard nodded before speaking. "So I'm assuming that you're not going to help me out with getting one of the girls, are you?"

There was a flash of light or something then he felt himself falling back. Reaching out, trying to grab onto whatever he could to keep himself from getting hurt, Howard was sure that there were wolves chasing him out of the restaurant. Then nothing.

Chapter 3

"So you went there and told him not only that I have three daughters but also that you're going to kill him if he came near them. Oh, and coming near me. What part of that do you think pisses me off more, Jeffery? The fact that you told him I had girls or the fact that you lied to him about killing him? Tell me because this might be the last time you get to ever open your mouth." Jeffery lowered his head and told her that he was sorry. "Look at me, you jackass and answer the fucking question."

"I was trying to warn him off so that he'd leave you alone." She asked him how that had worked out for him. "I don't think he's going to back off now. I think, and this is just me spitballing, that he might well be more determined. Because of me."

"Yes. Because now he knows that I have girls, right?" He told her that he'd wanted to buy one of them. "I'm sure you've told him that I wasn't going to do that, correct? You didn't tell him that you'd get back with him about it, did you?"

"I made it clear to him that he wasn't going to get away with any br —" She told him to finish when he stopped in mid-sentence. "I don't remember what I said." Paige turned to his brother.

"Edwin, what did he tell him?" His brother looked at him before telling Paige that he'd threatened him with death if he tried anything stupid. "Well, that's like the pot calling the kettle black, don't you think? I think that you're all stupid for going behind my back and talking to a man that I've not seen in over six years. Christ, what made you think that I needed you to help me? Nothing did, that's what. You didn't help me at all. In fact, I think that it's safe to say that you made matters worse for me. What do you think?"

"I guess we did. But I wanted you not to worry about him coming around and taking one of them." She crossed her arms over her breasts and tapped her foot. Like his mom did when he'd disappointed her over something that he'd done. "I'm sorry. I only wanted to be your knight in shining armor. And I failed at it."

"You certainly did." She started pacing then, and he found himself mesmerized by the way her hips moved back and forth when she took a step. As she came towards him in her snit, he watched as her breasts bounced ever so slightly. The slap to his face was a shock but nothing that he didn't deserve from her. He was glad Edwin had left so he'd not see that he'd been caught at ogling Paige. "What do you think you're looking at?"

"The most beautiful woman I've ever seen put together perfectly." She just stared at him, and he couldn't help himself. Pulling her into his arms, he held her there while she stared up at him. "May I kiss you, Paige?"

"Yes." He leaned into her mouth. Before he could take what she had offered, she spoke again. "But this doesn't mean that I'm not still mad at you." Jeffery kissed her.

He only meant a small kiss. Just a brushing of his mouth, his lips over hers. But as soon as he touched her mouth with his, he knew that he needed more than a simple kiss. A little taste of her. Jeffery wanted it all.

He swept his tongue over her partially closed lips and was welcomed inside. Tasting her, knowing that she was his, was something that he'd not expected. Something that he'd...well, he didn't deserve. Pulling her closer to him, feeling all of her body against his, Jeffery slid his hand down her body to her firm bottom and pulled her closer. Christ, she —

"Gross."

"Eww. You're kissing our mom."

"Are you using your tongue too?" The girls had found them.

Pulling away but not releasing Paige, he looked over at who he hoped would be his daughters soon. Winking at the three of them, it was Amy that winked back. The other two were making gagging sounds and pretending to put their fingers down their throat. Jeffery let Paige go and turned to look at the little girls that had come to mean so very much to him already.

"You're mom is upset with me." Amy told him that it didn't look like it. "Yes, well, I was trying to make her happy again. What do you think?"

"By kissing her? That's just too gross, Jeffery. Yuck." He looked at Paige when she cleared her throat. "Mom, we came to talk to you about something. It's important."

He knew that Amy was the oldest of the three of them by four minutes. He'd been told that several times over the last few days. Libby was the second oldest, and Glory was the third oldest. There was no youngest in this group. They were the oldest by birth. Amy was the most outspoken he knew.

"I have something to talk to the three of you about too. But we're going to calmly sit down and talk about it without throwing anyone under the bus." He wasn't sure what that meant until the three girls glared at Libby. "Whatever has happened, we're not going to make any one person responsible for whatever happened. Correct?"

"What if she is responsible? I mean, neither Glory nor I did it." Paige pointed to the living room. As they were walking away, he heard Amy say they should have him kiss her again so it would distract her. He stood up smiling. But that slid off his face when he faced Paige again.

"We need to talk as well." He nodded. "Also, you need to tell the girls about Howard. Not what you did. That's not anything that I want them to know about. But that he might be lurking around every corner. I'm worried for them."

"As am I. I swear to you, Paige. I never meant for this to turn out this way." She nodded, and he turned her face toward him. "I swear to you. He'll not get any of them. And if he does slip by me, I will get them back. I swear this on my mother's heart. But you need to remember all of you are immortal. All right? All four of you."

"Yes, I remember. But I'm their mother, and I worry. I'm sure that any one of the females in this family would say the same." He said that he knew that they would. "All right. This is going to be hard on me. But I want you to adopt them. I'm guessing that we should get married first. I don't want Howard to have any reason for the courts to take them away from me. And I figured that being married and your daughters too will give me a hand up."

"I swear to you, Paige, it will be in name only until you say differently." She eyed him, and he felt like she was looking for something, anything, to make it so she could call it off. When she turned and told him to follow her, Jeffery felt like his entire body had been slapped around and didn't come out on top. Following her into the living room, he felt as if he needed a long nap. But this was more important than anything that he'd ever done before. Reassuring his new family that he was there for them no matter what.

He was surprised to see Storm and Rain in the room with the girls. They had been talking about kissing, of all things. Just as he sat down on the couch with Paige, the two women turned and looked at them. He braced himself for whatever they had to say. It was Storm who spoke first.

"I've taken care that the two of you are married. That doesn't mean that you can't have a large wedding later if you wish, but with the things that are going on right now, we figured that it was safer for all of you that you were wedded. Also, after talking with the girls here, we'll take care that they're adopted by Jeffery. They are now Griffin's. Not that we didn't think they were when we found out that the two of you are mates, but it, again, will be better for what Howard might come up with in his bid to take one of them from you."

He didn't even ask how they knew that. His daughters—he loved the sound of that, had about a dozen questions each, asking them of anyone in the room that would answer until Rain raised her hand. The silence was profound. But it was just what was needed to calm things down.

"I know that you have questions. We do as well. But I'm going to leave the reasons for this up to your parents to answer questions. But I will tell you this. You must, under any circumstances, listen to what they have to say to you. If not, then there will be consequences that will harm you. Not kill you, but you will be hurt if you don't do as you're told when you're told. It's imperative that you understand that. All right?" All three of them nodded and told Rain that they'd do that. Then Libby asked about their mom. "She'll be hurt as well, but I want you to know that you will not lose her. None of you will die."

"What do you mean? Of course, we'll die." Amy looked at him, then back at Rain. "We have to die sometime, don't we?"

"You won't. Your father has been around for thousands of years. As have your grandparents. Again, I'll leave that up to them to answer. However, I can't say this enough, you must listen to them and anyone else in this family when it comes to keeping you safe." Rain got down on her knees in front of the girls. "You need only to think of us, and you can speak to us in your mind. If you are ever in trouble, think that you are, or even have a question for us, just think of the person, and they'll answer you. No matter if you think the question or even the thought of you being followed is silly, we're there for you. All right?"

"This sounds serious. I guess you're dumping it down for us because you think we can't handle it. But we can. Just tell us what you know." Amy looked at her sisters before turning back to Rain. "We're six, but we've been through a lot in all our lives. If you don't tell us, like my mom says, then you can't expect us to be prepared for whatever you know."

"All right. Straight shooters. I like that. Your father, the biological one, is set to take one of you. He might even try to take all three of you, for all I know right now. He's already offered Jeffery money to buy one, and as you know, he turned him down and warned him off. He's gunning to take one of you so that his wife, a dumbass if you ask me, wants a daughter." Amy asked if there was anything that they could do to make him not want them. "Doubtful. He's a man that wants to make his wife happy. Not because he loves her or even respects her, but because she holds all the money."

"That's just dumb." Rain agreed with Libby. "Okay, thank you, Dad, for not selling us. Sometimes I don't know why mom hasn't sold us off."

They all laughed. He even felt better after a little bit of the tension. Then he realized that Libby had called him Dad. It was almost too much for him to think about. When she smiled at him, Jeffery could have taken on the world and didn't even care if he won or lost the fight. He was a dad to someone. To three someones.

As Rain and Storm answered questions, he interjected answers when he had them. Like they'd be living in his home from now on if that was what Paige wanted. And thankfully, she did. There was a bedroom for each of them, and yes, it had been set up for them. Storm told them too about the pack school if that was someplace they wanted to go and set up a time with Paige to go and look it over.

He had his list of things that he was to do and to look into. The things that he had to do weren't that difficult—finding out if one of his brothers could check out the girls before going to school this year, as well as finding a car for Paige that had enough room for the six of them. Apparently, they were going to include Drew in all their activities so he could be better acquainted with his cousins and aunt. Jeffery thought that was a splendid idea.

Jeffery was happy that he'd started carrying

around a pad of paper all the time after getting the government job that he had. They would generally call him in the middle of the night with information, and he found it better to have written things down rather than to try and be awake to remember everything. When he was ready to put his pad away, it was Glory that took it from him and wrote on the next page. He looked at it when she handed it back to him.

"Thank you for this. I'd hate to have missed these dates." It was not just their birthday with the times they were born but also their mom's birthday. The girls' birthday was still some time away, but Paige was born on Christmas Eve. Not a date that he'd forget. However, he was glad to have it written down. Before putting the pad away, he wrote down today's date as his wedding anniversary so he'd know that too. Who knew that having a family could be so much fun.

~*~

Paige wasn't sure what possessed her to think that taking four kids to the mall was a good idea. Not that the kids were being all that disruptive, but she was on the lookout for Howard so much that she was stressing too much to have fun. When Luna joined them in the store, devoted to everything back to school, she could have cried. Stressed out and overwrought, Paige went willingly with her when she suggested getting some lunch with the kids.

"You look terrible." Paige told her daughter not to be rude. "Well, you do. You look like you've been sucking on an all-day lemon, and you didn't like it. You need to take a chill pill, Mom. Or start drinking. Holly's mother drinks a lot. She calls it adult juice, but I can smell it. It smells like Mr. Hopewell does when he came to the house last time."

"I have no intentions of drinking. What a thing to say to me, Glory." She'd noticed that Glory had started being more outgoing all the time, and she loved it. "All right. You can have want you want to eat, but what is the rule? You have to eat what you order."

She noticed that Luna was enjoying the kids. It occurred to her that she treated all the kids the same. Like they were the best thing she'd ever encountered. When Charlie joined them, too, she had a feeling that something was going on. It had her looking around for Howard.

"He's not here, love." She nodded at Charlie. "We just decided that since we were in town, we'd come and have some fun with you guys. Also, we have a list of school supplies that their teachers gave to us. Allen said you were buying Drew's for him as well."

"Yes. He's working at the pack house today, and I told him that I'd get them. Jeffery is working with some top-secret thing for the government, and I thought that if I got out of the house, we'd not disturb him so much." Charlie told her that Jeffery rarely lets things disturb him when he's working, but he could see the distraction with having four beautiful women around. "Thank you for that, kind sir. We've been settling into the house. It's huge, isn't it? I mean, even with the girls all having their own rooms, there is still a lot of space left over."

"I believe at one time that was a hotel. I think they might have even had a hand in building it as well. When it came up for sale, we were going to buy it and turn it into a hotel again. But Jeffery decided that he wanted to see if he could turn it into a home. I think he worked on it by himself for a long time before he just hired a company to do it for him. I think it turned out really nice, don't you? I mean, the kitchen alone is wonderful."

Paige agreed with Luna. Helping the girls order

at the restaurant, she was amazing every time they read something that they were old enough to do that. It was the little things, yes, but she was surprised by it. She had to laugh when the waitress looked at her when Libby ordered.

"You want a steak sandwich? It comes with onions and peppers, you know that, don't you, honey?" Libby told her that if she could see her way in giving her extra onions and peppers that she'd be happy. "All right. I'm guessing that you want the pepper jack cheese too."

"Oh yes, ma'am, I do. The hotter, the better." Amy ordered the same thing but wanted sriracha sauce to add to it, and Glory, her baby, said that she wanted hers to have sliced tomatoes as well as avocado on hers. As well as the hot things her sister had ordered. Paige loved her girls.

"Well, I'm thinking that these girls can out hot their uncle. Stone loves all things hot. A few years ago, he took a trip to some European country and brought back this hot sauce that could only be stored in glass. He told us it was so hot that it would melt through plastic. I didn't believe him, of course, but it sure did burn the hairs in my nose when I took a sniff of it." Paige told him that the girls didn't get to have hot meals like this one very often. They'd been on a budget for so long. "You just hit up that uncle of yours, and I'm sure that he'd take the three of you out just to watch you eat. He'll love every moment of it. What are you getting, Drew? Hot stuff too?"

"No thanks. I'll just take a regular hamburger with cheese, not hot and French fries, please." When he asked for a malt with his meal, everyone ordered one as well. "I'd like a chocolate made with chocolate ice cream, please." Again, everyone got the same thing, including Charlie and Luna.

Paige felt so much better after eating. Nothing like her daughters did, but she liked hot things too. Once they were all finished up, each of them enjoying their sammich, as Luna called it, they set off for shopping again. With the two extra people there, it made shopping with the four kids much easier on her stress level.

It felt good to be able to let the girls pick out more than one outfit for themselves. Drew had become the one to tell them if the dresses would pass the rules at the school. They could change into whatever they wanted, but they wanted to be able to pick out the dresses that they'd gotten too. She also noticed that they weren't buying the same outfits anymore. Not that she minded too much, but she had enjoyed dressing them all alike.

Once they were finished, as far as she was concerned shopping for school, she pulled out her list of things that were needed for the house. It wasn't all that much, but they did need towels, a lot of them, as it turned out. There were toiletries for the girls as well as things for Drew for both his home and when he came to stay with them. She thought that Drew would be spending a lot of time with them during the school year as they were going to be driven in by her or Jeffery. She was glad that he'd be close too.

Luna and Charlie took the kids with them when they finished up so that she could handle the grocery store on her own. She didn't have any idea what to get for Jeffery and decided that if he wanted anything different than the girls, she'd pick it up for him. By the time she was finished up with that, she was glad that she had a larger car with a big back end for all the things that she'd picked up.

It had been so long since she could afford to buy two kinds of cereal for the girls instead of buying the cheapest bag of whatever was on sale. She was able to afford to get them tea bags, a big deal for the four of them when they were living alone to have a nice cup of tea on cooler mornings. She had noticed that Jeffery liked a cup, too, but he wanted black tea instead of green.

There were other perks that she enjoyed while shopping. Just being able to not have to keep track of every penny so she'd not have to put things back when she got to the register made her day. Being able to have meat for every meal was wonderful too. Not having to purchase large jars of peanut butter was all right with her as well. In fact, after pulling a jar off the shelf and putting it in the cart, she put it back before moving away. No more peanut butter for a long time was all right with her too.

The girls and Drew helped her bring the things in. It was exciting for the girls to help unload the bags of things that she'd gotten. It hurt her heart a little when they were excited about having name-brand salad dressing rather than the cheap stuff they all hated. Also, the brand of cookies that she bought for them as an afternoon snack was a better buy for her since they were happy that they weren't oily.

"Ms. Jenkins was here a little while ago." Luna helped by folding up the bags that she'd brought home. "She'll be the cook here. Although she can't start until Monday, the girls have given her a rundown on things that the household doesn't care for. Or things that they're not allowed to have. I think you've made good choices for being on a budget for so long."

"We were broke, not on a budget." Luna laughed. "I have to admit, I'm glad for a cook. I told Jeffery that I needed to work at something, or I'd go crazy waiting for them to come home from school. I can't believe that they're going to be in first grade already. We're going to see the pack school in the morning if everything goes according to plan."

"Rarely does anything going to plan happen around here." Luna and Charlie left not long after the groceries were put away. Drew also made his way home as it was getting close to the time that Allen would be coming home. He told her that they should make plans to come over tomorrow night for a cookout to celebrate everything. She told him that she'd talk to Allen. Drew hugged them all goodbye when he left. Then it was just the four of them.

"Now, what do we do?" They ended up doing the laundry to get the towels washed for tomorrow. Her daughters had never been bath sort of kids, and she was glad that their rooms all had showers for them to use. Putting away the towels, Paige was also grateful to find that they each had their own personal things in their room, things that she was sure one of the others had gotten for them.

Jeffery told her that he wasn't going to be home until after nine that night. So she made dinner for just the four of them after hearing from Jeffery. After putting the girls to bed and making sure that the house was locked up, Paige sat in the living room, reading a book with the fireplace going. It was something that she'd not had an opportunity to do for a long time.

She must have dozed off at some point. The book wasn't anything that she was enjoying anyway, and was awakened by her cell phone ringing. Looking at the time on it, she was surprised to find that it was nearly ten. Answering the phone, she was shaken all the way awake by the voice at the other end screaming at her.

"Shut up." Whoever it was, she had a feeling it was Howard. They were screaming at her about something she couldn't make out. When it was quiet at the other end, she sat up straighter on the couch and reached out for whoever was close to tell them what was going on. "Now, tell me who this is and what you want."

"It's fucking Howard, you stupid slut. Where the hell are you?" She told him that she was home, reading a good book. "Oh? I'm at the apartment where you're supposed to be, and there isn't hide nor hair of you. So again, where the hell are you?"

"I'm at my home reading a good book. Why do you care, Howard? We've not spoken for nearly seven years. What do you want? In the event it might have slipped your mind, it's kind of late for a social call." Jeffery told her that he was pulling into the driveway but that Edwin had sent pack to the house. She thanked him. Paige realized that she'd missed something when Howard wasn't speaking. "I wasn't paying attention to you, Howard. Will you please say whatever it is you have to say and hang up? I have a big day tomorrow getting my children registered for school."

"They're my kids too. I want you to hand over one of them so that I can placate my wife. She's got it in her head that she wants a daughter. Why, you might ask? I don't know, and I don't give a good shit, either. But you're going to do it, or so help me, I'll make you regret meeting me." She told him that she had always regretted that other than the fact that he'd given her such lovely daughters. That what he was saying wasn't much of a threat to her since she knew that he was an idiot. "You don't have any right to be calling me shit."

"I didn't call you shit, dummy, but that's a good name for you too. You tell Rachel if she wants another child by you, why she'd want to have sex with you is beyond me, but if she wants another child, then she'll have to do it the old-fashioned way. Having sex. You're not going to go anywhere near my children." He said that he'd take them from her as he was better fit anyway. He also told her that he'd been snipped. Whatever the hell that meant. "I doubt that you could prove that in a court of law. I'm married, and my husband has adopted them to be his own."

Jeffery came into the room with her, and she took his hand into hers. It was like a lifeline, and she was never as happy to have it as she was at that moment. Paige realized that Howard was calling her not just a liar but also a slut when Jeffery put out his hand for the phone. She gladly handed it over.

"Howard?" She heard Howard sputtering at the other end of the line. "Yes, that's you unless you're too stupid to remember your name. What are you doing calling my wife at this hour? Do you know that our daughters will be up soon, and you disturbing her rest is going to make her cranky in the morning. It takes a lot of time and energy to get *our* daughters up and going. You should—"

"Listen here, you moron. I tried to be nice about this, and now I'm pissed off. My wife is making me come home, and she told me that I'd better not be without her daughter. I'm thinking that I'm going to take all three of them away from Paige—I no more believe that you two are married and that you adopted those brats than I do I fathered them. But you'll do as you're told, or I'm going to make you regret messing with me. Do you hear me?"

"Yes." That's all Jeffery said, and Paige found that to be hysterical. When Jeffery didn't say anything else, she had to put her hand over her mouth in order to not laugh out loud. She wasn't ready to have Howard so pissed off that he came to their home.

"What do you mean, 'yes'? I asked you a question." Jeffery said that he'd answered it too. "You're going to regret this, moron."

"You like calling people names, don't you? I mean, not only have you called my wife names but me as well. You know that shows a low intellect, don't you? But as for you taking my daughters, that's not going to happen. They're in a good home, and they're happy. Something that I'm sure would never have happened had you been a part of their life. Also, I don't know if you're aware of this or not, but you can't claim that they're your daughters and that they're not in the same breath. It makes you sound like you're a little off your noodle." Jeffery closed the connection and looked at her. "We're going to sue him as soon as tomorrow. For threats. However, I have a feeling that he's going to be telling the judge all kinds of shit that isn't true, or perhaps it is true, and he'll say that he offered to buy one of the girls, and that won't go over well."

"How do we prove that?" He told her that he had help in high places. "Unless it's the president, I'm thinking that we're going to be screwed." He just smiled at her. "You know the president?"

"I do. As does my entire family. Not only will we win, love, but he'll be in jail until our daughters are out of college and have a family of their own." She liked the sound of that. "All right. I have some more work to do tonight. Then I'll have tomorrow off so that we can go to the pack school early."

She was headed up to bed when she realized that she wanted to sleep with Jeffery by her side. Not only that, but she decided that it was well past time that they made love. Paige found herself thinking about that a great deal as she readied for sleep. Tomorrow, she thought, she was going to jump his bones and show him what nearly seven years of celibacy can do to a woman with needs. Laughing to herself, she got into bed and fell fast asleep. Not having any worries could do that to a person was her final thought.

Chapter 4

Jeffery was in a terrible mood. It was mainly the man that he was working with. The guy that was supposed to be taking out the target that he had pinpointed for him. Right up to the point of describing what the man had on.

"Look, I don't see him. I can't get to what I can't see." Putting the headphones on mute, he growled. Even his wolf was getting frustrated, and that was never a good thing. "I'm going to call it. There is no one—"

"You do that, and I'll have you before a firing squad in ten minutes. The fucking man is standing not four feet from you. I can see you, and you fucking should be able to see him. Green shirt with the words 'FUCK USA' on it. He has on a pair of khaki shorts that are navy blue. His fucking left shoe is untied. Does that narrow it down for you?"

Jeffery took in a deep breath, then let it out slowly, counting to ten four times. When someone touched his mind, he snarled at them to go the fuck away. He heard Edwin laugh. That didn't help his mood one bit, and he told him that.

I can feel your anger. Want me to pop you there so you can show the idiot the man? I'm reasonably sure that I can find him with what I've heard you telling him. I can do that now. Jeffery told his older brother that he wasn't helping at all. *I know that, dummy. I'm trying to keep you from blowing a fuse. Just let me come over there, and I'll talk you down. It's not doing you a bit of good to yell at the idiot at the other end of your mike. By the way, does Paige know what you do for a living? Other than putting in cable and satellites for people?*

No. I've not even told our parents. Though I think Dad might know. He's been hinting around about me telling him for a few years now." He spoke to the idiot that he was guiding toward the target. When he suddenly found the man, it was over before he could tell him good job. As he got out of the network that had found the man, he continued speaking to his brother. *I love having a family, you know. But I do* miss being about to just come and go as I please. I think it's mostly to do with this job. I'm beginning to hate it more than before. I think it has to do with a lot of things nowadays. It's just too easy, my job.

No, I think it's not too easy. It's you that would think that. No one else could do what you do and do it well. I know that you've had all kinds of awards that you can't talk about. The last time that you took me with you, I was amazed…well, not so much amazed as I was proud of you. Christ, Jeffery, you've saved this country more than anyone else has. He thanked his big brother, not sure how to respond to his praise. I can see you now. You're sitting at your desk, looking around to see if anyone else heard me talking to you about how proud I am of you. Aren't you?

Kinda. He heard his phone ringing just as he was getting up from the chair. I have another job. Christ, can't anyone just be good for a change? Come over in about an hour. You and I will take a long good run and see if we can find the path that Mom was talking about the other night that she used to find mushrooms on. All right?

After getting things ready to hang out with Edwin, he felt better. Not great, but a good deal more than he had before. Answering the call, he was happy that he had a different handler on the end of the call.

It took him twenty minutes to locate who he was to take care of before he found her. The handler on the other end found her a few seconds later. However, it wasn't a shot that he was willing to make. She was with a group of other women, and they seemed to be too close for comfort for either of them. He was going to get a clean shot of her before they were to leave the restaurant. He had plenty of time to wait on her. While waiting, he looked for Howard and his wife.

Since he'd found his mate, Jeffery was having a hard time thinking about killing a woman when he was working. But the file that came up on his computer told him all he needed to know about her, and he didn't have that problem for long. Even finding out about her destruction had him thinking that he was in the wrong business.

Howard was right where he'd been for the last three hours. At the police station. Mores the pity that he wasn't in jail but free to roam around. Jeffery did wonder if he knew that his wife had arrived at his hotel but didn't care enough to let it bother him. The two of them were going to be served at five today, and he couldn't be happier about it.

It was Storm, with the help of Edwin, that had

gotten the paperwork set up for him and Paige. They were harassing them by calling and threatening to take their children. Lucky for him, when Howard had called, Edwin had set his and Paige's phone to be recorded. Magically, of course, but it was caught of him telling them both that he wasn't going to be messing with them much longer and that he might well take the three girls. Over his dead body.

And since he couldn't die, he was just as happy for Howard to end up pushing daisies. However that saying went, he was all for it. Upon looking into the background of his wife, Rachel, he wasn't any more thrilled with her background than he was with Howards. She was nearly as bad as the woman that he was targeting right now.

She'd been arrested several times, a total of fourteen times, for leaving the scene of an accident. Hit and run seemed to be her way of getting out of paying up. Because every time she went before the courts, she was given a fine, one that he couldn't find that she paid and sent on her merry way. Also, and this one boggled his mind that she was getting away with, she had raided her employees' pension funds four times with four different businesses over the last eight years. Also, there was a notation on her file that she'd never paid unemployment taxes, federal taxes that she took out of their checks as well as their health insurance. He wondered how her employees felt when they showed up at the hospital and were told they didn't have any coverage, not even a little bit.

She had also known about Paige and her struggle to make ends meet when she'd been living with the girls. According to what he'd been able to find out, she bragged about it to her 'friends' at the country club. Two of the women that she had told had hired Paige to help out when they really didn't need her. Just to help her out.

"I have her. It's done." He thanked the guy and watched as he blended into the crowd that had gathered around the dead woman. "I'm headed to my safe house. If you need me, you know where I am."

After signing off with the soldier, he watched Howard as he left the station. He was headed to the hotel where his wife was currently at with their son. Jeffery thought that the kid was a sickly-looking little guy. Even for being twelve years old, he looked younger than his daughters. He wished that he had the idea to of hacked into the hotel lobby, but he'd been pushing things to the limit today. After signing off, he heard from Paige.

I have a job. She laughed, and he was glad for that. It lifted his downed spirits up a great deal. *I'm going to be working for your mom and dad on a couple of projects that they have going. Also, the pack has decided that I'd make a good substitute teacher for them, and I'm going to do that part-time. I think I'll feel better about being able to keep an eye on the kids that way. What are you doing?*

I've been watching Howard. His wife is in town with their kid. He told her what he thought about the little boy. *Also, the two of them are going to be served with a court hearing on their threats to us. Just so you know, we're going to owe Edwin big time for getting this pushed through for us.*

Anything that he wants. She asked him about what he thought was going to happen to them. *I mean, at the very least, I'm thinking that they'll have to serve some jail time, right? It's the least that can happen to them, I hope.*

Edwin is under the impression that they'll both end up doing time for the threats. And once it's figured out that the girls are biologically his, then he'll owe you back child support. Not that we need it, but it will be great to have him pay it. We can have it put back for the girls to use when they get older. She asked him how much he thought it would be. *It will be based on their income. More than likely, it'll be around five hundred a month, times three. Over the last six or so years, that could be a nice savings for them. Then he'll have to pay it until they're eighteen. Just a guess on that, however.*

That'll be wonderful for the girls. She told him, too, that she'd had a DNA test done on the girls when they were born. *I don't know what possessed me to do that, but I have them. So when I went on that website that has DNA to find relatives when you could join for free, Howard was on there. There were about ten kids on there that matched his nearly one hundred percent.*

I'll have to join that and get those for the hearing. He and his little family are going to be broke paying out child support on all his kids, I think. They both laughed. *Okay, I'm in. Let me have a look around here for a minute.* He found not only Howard's name, but now there were fourteen matches to his DNA, one of them being his son. Telling Paige what he'd been able to find, she seemed glad.

Paige laughed. Just talking to her made him feel less stressed. He supposed that was the way it was supposed to be with a mate and was glad that she was his. Jeffery had noticed that his brothers were all more relaxed than they used to be. Especially Edwin. Who had been so tense about little stuff that everyone was avoiding him.

"I'll be home soon. I have to tell you, it's wonderful having a car that I can get the girls in. Most of the time, we walked everywhere. Even when it was too cold." She told him that she loved him dearly and then closed the connection. Jeffery sat there at his desk for a good half hour just thinking about the fact that Paige loved him.

Getting up, he was excited to see the girls coming home. They'd been at the pack school most of the day, and he had a feeling that they loved it. While he made them a snack to hold them over until dinner, they told him all the things that they were going to learn. It was things like being able to find their way home by looking at the stars and trees and things that they could eat while out and about.

"That sure would have been nice when we were poor." The others laughed, but it hurt him a little that they'd been without more than they had. However, they were adjusting well, and he thought that was better than anything.

After they were finished up with their snack

of apples and milk, they wanted to go into the yard to explore. He was ready to remind them again to be careful when the three of them, in unison, repeated the thing that they said to them every time they went outside. To be aware of their surroundings.

As he and the new cook decided on dinner, he was thrilled to have someone doing that messy part for them. While he didn't mind cooking on occasion, he didn't want to do it every night. Going into the yard to see what the girls had unearthed, he was happy that they were taking this so seriously. That didn't mean that he wasn't still worried about them, but it made it easier for him to allow them some time alone.

By the time Paige had made it home, they had found some worms and mushrooms that weren't something that they could eat and moss on the trees. Jeffery was very proud of them when they also knew that it could mean the difference between life and death for someone with them while lost in the woods. Paige listened to everything that they had to say to her again, and he laughed when Libby got upset that she'd not been able to tell her mom first about the moss on the rocks.

Dinner was wonderful. Beef tips over

homemade noodles and warm bread. There were salads too that they all enjoyed. Even a dessert of apple brown Betty with ice cream was a special treat. If he'd been in charge of dinner, they would have gone out. But this was so much nicer in that they had the privacy to talk to each other.

The girls were nearly falling asleep on their chairs as dinner plates were cleared away. Taking them up to bed, he was able to read the first page of their book when they were out. Taking the others to their beds, they'd ended up in Libby's room tonight. He kissed them on the forehead and was glad that they'd told him how much they loved him. Jeffery felt himself doing a bit of a jig on his way down the stairs with Paige.

"How about you and I go to bed together. I'm not entirely sure I can do sex, but—" He asked her, trying to keep a straight face of what doing sex was. "You know. Having sex. I'm exhausted, and I don't think I'll enjoy it as much as I want to."

"You will. But I understand. I'm exhausted too. Work kicked my ass." She said that the excitement was what got her, and the two of them locked up the house and went up to the bedroom that she'd been sleeping in. For himself, he could have made love to her all night, but she'd already put out the rules, and he was going to abide by them even if it killed him. And immortal or not, he was sure that he was going to suffer badly for this.

~*~

Jeffery was sound asleep when he realized that someone was screaming. Leaping out of the bed, his wolf took him as he crashed open the door and headed down the hall. The only bedroom door that was open was the one at the end. As he wasn't entirely sure which one of the girls' bedrooms that was, he raced there as the screaming continued.

All three of the girls were there. Pausing at the doorway, his wolf suddenly unsure, he watched until they noticed him. Moving deeper into the room, he got up on the bed, his wolf nuzzling Amy as she cried. He nearly told Paige that he had then when he noticed the look of absolute terror on her face too. When she came into the room, Amy was hugging him while she told the four of them what she'd been screaming about.

"I thought he was here. Right here in my room, hurting me. Mr. Murry was trying to tear me away from you guys while I was yelling at him to stop. He kept telling me that he was going to be a better father than all the fathers in the world." Amy continued to cry as she told them that he'd hurt her legs and arms so badly. "And he said that his money was better and that he had more. I don't know why that should matter at all. We didn't have any money, but Mom loved us all to pieces because we were family. I don't want him as my family, Dad. Can you make him go away, please?"

Licking the small wounds that looked like she'd done herself by trying to claw her demons away from her, Amy hugged him again. When the girls gathered around their mother, he swiftly shifted from wolf to man with his clothing on in seconds. Gathering on the floor with them, he held Amy in his arms.

"What part of your bad dream bothered you the most? Him taking you or the part he was a better father? I'd like to know that." Amy said it was that his money was better. "I don't know how money is better either. Unless he thought that he had more of it. He doesn't. I don't even have to know how much he has to know that we have a great deal more."

"How much?" He smiled at Glory when her mother scolded her. "Well, these are things that a girl has to know, Mom. I mean, I'd like to go to college someday. Can we afford for me to go and not have to work too much? Sammy's sister was going to college, and she was messing up by having to make her ends meet. Not sur what that means either, as we never had our means lining up ever, but I think she was messing her grades up because she was working too hard. Are we going to have to do that?" Jeffery smiled.

"How much do you think would be a lot of money? I mean, you said Mr. Murry was telling you that he had better money. Let's assume that he meant more. How much do you think he might have with his wife that would make you think he had a great deal?" Each of them gave a number that they thought was a lot of money. "Millions of dollars is a lot of money. Even a hundred thousand is a lot of money for a lot of people. But we have more than that. Millions upon millions that add up to billions and billions of money."

"Your whole family has billions? That is a lot of money." She turned to her mom again. "I won't have to work at all but do good in class, Mom. Ain't that wonderful?"

"It is wonderful, but I don't think that's what he's saying to you, honey." Glory turned to look at him, and he told her that they, as a little family had billions of dollars. "You girls know that you can't go bragging about how much money is in this household, don't you? You know it will make people want to take you just to get a piece of his money. Right?"

"It's our money. All five of us. And if we have any more children, it will be there as well. And yes, Glory, I want you to go anywhere you want to study and not have to worry about working. I have several degrees that have served me well over the decades. I've been a doctor, an attorney. Even a businessman that helped others. I think that Edwin was a surgeon before he was in the service. I know that Harman has been a writer of children's books. He made clothing for a while. Even Mom and Dad have had their hand in other things other than just being our parents."

"They have money, too, don't they?" Jeffery explained that they all had a good deal of wealth, but the trick was not to let anyone else know about it like their mother had said so that they don't try and take it from them. "I know that too. Everyone at school only wanted to be friends with Delight Morgan—a goofy name if you ask me— when her daddy was sending things to the classroom for us to eat and snack on. Not me. I didn't care for the things that he was sending in. Mom said that they were too surgery, so I didn't eat them. Not that I was being jealous like they said, I just don't care for a lot of sweets. Your momma does, Dad. But not me. Anyway, when her daddy went to jail on some kind of dirty money stuff, there were no more snacks. Everyone treated her differently, didn't they, Amy?"

"They did. I ate the snacks, but I was polite to her about them. Thanking her and telling her to thank her dad for us. Nobody else was. They were complaining about how there was things in the bag that they didn't like." Amy rolled her eyes. "Like grandda says, you can't please everyone, so there is no point in even trying. Anyway, when the stuff stopped, she didn't have any more friends but us three. We didn't like her much, but we weren't rude about it. Do you think you're going to jail for dirty money, Dad?"

"No." Jeffery laughed. "I got my money the legal way. All of us did. By hard work and making sound investments. And it's not dirty money but money laundering. I remember that case. It was all over the news that Morgan Insurance was caught helping out the mob by exchanging their money out for good cash. I'll explain that when you're a bit older and can understand it better."

"Good because I don't." They talked about the nightmare off and on. He wasn't sure how they'd found out about Howard talking about his money being better, but he thought it brought home the fact that you didn't talk about how much money you might have in your accounts if you didn't want people to have a chunk of it. He'd learned that from his father.

"I'm hungry." He was as well and asked Glory what she wanted to eat. "I don't want cold pizza ever again in my life, just so you know. And no donuts. Or bagels. Why people think that is a good breakfast food when you don't have any money is beyond me."

He laughed at their antics as the three of them kept on their jammies while they all five headed down the stairs. He was still worried about Amy. She put on a brave front, but she was hurting, he thought, in ways that he couldn't reach. Knowing that this ending of the Murry's going to jail would have a big effect on all of them, he was hoping that she'd soon understand that no one was going to touch any of them while he was alive.

He had come to know that the girls, even though they looked alike, were as different as snowflakes.

While Glory, who was coming out of her shell as well as Libby was, liked bacon, she hated sausage unless it was in gravy. And even then, she'd pick out the meat and put it on Amy's plate. Libby didn't care for bacon. She would eat sausage links but not patties. That one he could understand as he had the same preference. Amy loved all breakfast meats and would end up with her sisters' leftovers on her plate before the end of the meal.

Fried eggs weren't as big a hit as he had thought they'd be. They liked pancakes and would eat them, but they liked waffles even more. And aebleskiver, Danish pancake balls were their favorite. His, too, when they were filled with his mom's raspberry jam. He thought he could eat them at every meal.

They were finishing up breakfast and the clean-up when his mom showed up. She'd been going to make them breakfast before they had to go to school for a project. He noticed how dejected she looked, but it was Libby that told her that next time she could cook for them. While he did a good job, she told her grandma, that Grandma added that extra something that made them so much better. He'd have to remember that Libby was the romantic one in the family from now on. She was a charmer too.

As they headed out the door, he got another phone call. This one was from the acting president of the United States. He wanted him to take care of someone for him. As he was getting settled in his office, the email that he used came up. Before he could read past the second word, Storm popped into the room with Edwin.

"They want me to kill off the former president." Handing them a copy of the email, he read the rest of the email to himself. When he got to the part where it told what was going on with the man, he decided that this was well above his pay grade. He said as much to the current president.

"I know you think that, Junkie but I need this done." No one knew who he was really, and he was glad for that. His brother and sister-in-law in the room with him were the only ones that knew his true identity when it came to working with the government. Junkie had been a moniker when he'd been working to make some money for a charity that he'd founded. Now it was all he used. "There is a substantial pay for this work. The only two people that will be involved are myself and you. He's causing us a great deal of trouble where he is, and we need to get him out of the way."

"Why me?" Putting the secure landline on speaker, he let the other two in the room listen in. "I mean, I don't mind working with the government, but this is…well, he's not my usual workload."

"No, he's not. However, if you wait for the file that I'm having sent to your box, you'll see what I'm talking about when I say he must be made to disappear. He knows things, things that only the president would know and understand, that he's sharing with others. The kind of others that we don't necessarily want to have knowing how our government works." Storm popped out and came back with the file. No one would ever know that she'd been the one to get it too. As the three of them looked over the paperwork, he saw what the other man was talking about. "He's made threats too that would cost us if anyone were to find out about them."

There were tapes of recorded conversations between Mike Waller and someone else. He'd know the voice anywhere as he'd been to their home a few times. Never as a direct threat but as a family friend. Until Mike was caught fucking things up by trying to start a war for the nice big income that would come with it. He'd even had plans of killing off Edwin and using him as a high-ranking officer that had gone bad.

Storm passed the file to Edwin and said, "If this is true, he needs to be gone." But finding out if it was true was something he couldn't do. "We can. I mean, it wouldn't take all that much for one of us to stick with him for a couple of days. It might not even take that long if he's talking to anyone that will listen. All that information needs to do is get not just in the wrong hands but out where someone with a grudge hears it. I'll go now. He'll never know that I'm there."

When she disappeared, he looked at Edwin. He was reading the file still, and he had to say Edwin's name three times before he looked at him. Jeffery asked him if he was all right.

"Not particularly. This man was going to kill my entire family for votes. I'd take him out right now for no other reason than that." He told Edwin that he'd do it for free for him. "Yes, well, when Storm gets back, we'll see what she can tell us. I can do it, but I'd better not. I'd not make it quick nor painless for the man. And I think people would know that I'd done it. I'd have my wolf tear him apart, and that would leave a lot to be investigated."

Storm was back in less than half an hour. She

told him that it was done and that she was happy to have done it. It would look like he'd killed himself, and that would be the end of it. No note as he'd not been able to have a pencil or paper. They both left as his email was popping up pictures of what Storm had done. He was thrilled it was over. And he'd bet that both Storm and Edwin wouldn't speak of this or anything to do with Waller ever again.

Chapter 5

Howard was pissed. Christ, oh mighty, his wife was making things more difficult than they needed to be. She'd been complaining about the hotel, the town, as well as how much time it was taking from her social clubs. Not that he understood that part. He knew for a fact that no one liked her any more than he did. Now they were in a courtroom full of people that he had no idea why he was there for. At this point, he just wanted to go home and put his feet up. Damn, Paige and her girls. This was costing him time and energy that he didn't want to be wasting on damned females.

When they were told to rise, he did so but took his time at it. He paid taxes, and he...well, his wife paid taxes, he guessed, and he was going to milk things for all he was worth.

He was, of course, reprimanded by the judge, but he told her that he'd forgotten that she was in charge. Again, he was told that she was in charge and for as much as she had going on today, he'd better be paying attention to the rules.

"Yes, ma'am." He sat down, then with a poke from Rachel, he stood up. "Ma'am, your honor? I'd like to know what this is all about. Paige there has my children, and she isn't sharing them with me. I think that I could do a better job raising them than she has anyway. Not that I want to be burdened with a bunch of girls, but you see, I'm trying to make my wife happy with getting her a girl to raise. What with the money my wife and I have, it should be a no-brainer for you to make her just hand one of them over. But Paige, she won't even sell me one of them."

"Excuse me. Did you just say she wouldn't sell you one of her daughters?" Howard nodded, thinking that her tone told him that she didn't believe it either. "You do know that it's considered a crime to try and buy someone's children, Mr. Murry. No matter what state you are from, that is a big no-no. Did she give you a reason for not wanting to sell one to you by any chance?"

"She had the nerve to tell me just no, your honor. Just like that is supposed to make it right. My wife here, Rachel, wants a little girl, like I've been saying and since, well, I'm not believing that I'm their father, but she says that I am, then Paige should hand one or two of them over. I want to make my wife happy, you see."

"I'm sure you need to with the things I've found out about you. Your wife as well, it seems. Neither of you has led a very good life law wise, have you, Mr. Murry?" He didn't know what she meant, and since she didn't say anything else to clear that up for him, he didn't either. "Mr. Murry, are you aware that you currently have several offspring that you've been neglecting? None of them are your wanted female children, but there are a few male children out there. Are you aware of this? In addition to not paying any kind of support for these children, you've not once seen them. Is that correct?"

"Sort of. I mean, I've been keeping a distant eye on them just to make sure that they're not causing me any trouble. But no, I've not—I'm not sure that any of them are even mine either, you see. There isn't any proof that they are." She asked her bailiff if he would hand over the paperwork that she'd been given by

Mr. Edwin Griffin, attorney for the little girls. "What's this? I didn't tell anyone that they could go around testing me for this? This is an attack of privacy, if you know what I mean."

"I have it here that you've been on a website that lets you search for people that might be related to you. Is that correct?" He told her that it was sort of fun to see. "Yes, well, there are fourteen children, all under the age of fifteen, that are a perfect match to your DNA. Also, and I'm not at all finding this hard to believe, you've been on each of those children's information at least three times a day since they were born. Of your body, I want to point out."

"Those can be rigged to make anyone think that they have a lot of kids out there. This doesn't mean a thing." She said that it was her rules again and that it meant everything. "Well, I don't believe it. As far as I'm concerned, there is only one child of mine, and it's sitting right here —" He looked around and asked his wife where their son was. "Well, he was supposed to be coming with us today. I wanted to show you that I'm a good father."

"Howie is in the hospital, your honor." He eyed the man that stood up and told the court where his son was. Mr. Riffing or something like that. "He was left alone in the hotel room and went to the front desk, telling them he didn't feel well. The manager tried to reach his parents with no hope of it, so they called an ambulance for him as he was getting sicker by the moment. He's currently in intensive care with a high fever as well as congestion in his lungs. The doctor on duty said that he'd been ill like this for about two weeks. That he thought that someone might have noticed before then."

"Mr. or Mrs. Murry? Were you aware that your son was ill when you left him alone in the hotel you're currently staying in? And why did it take a stranger to you having to tell you where your little boy was?" Howard told the judge that it was women's work. "I see. I don't, but in an effort to save time here, I want you to know that this isn't showing either of you in a good light right now."

"He complains all the time. It's either he's sick with something, or he's sleepy all the time. I just gave up on trying to keep up with all his illnesses." The judge looked at Rachel, so he did as well. Howard wondered what she was seeing because he wasn't seeing a thing wrong with his wife. When she continued talking about their boy, he looked up at the judge. She had to understand how hard it was when all your kid did was whine about shit all the time. She was a woman, after all. "Just the other day, he told me that he was going to throw up. I sent his little ass outside so that he could do it there. Christ, I'm not cleaning up puke. Not when I was ready to go out again."

"So you're telling me that you left your son, a minor, on his own when he told you how ill he was?" Rachel glanced at him and then nodded at the judge. He heard someone snickering in the back and turned to look at what was going on. One of the girls was laughing. He asked her what was so fucking funny. "Mr. Murry. You'll watch your language in my courtroom. And I will be asking the questions. However, in this incident, I can understand part of the laughter. Ms. Griffin, I presume? What is it you find funny? Please share it with the courts. I think I could use a good laugh myself about now."

"My mom and dad would have called an ambulance right away if any one of us said we wasn't feeling good." The little girl stood up on her chair and looked at him and his wife. "You're not a good person, Mr. Murry. Not at all. I wouldn't want you to be my father even if you was the last one on this earth. To think that you left your son all by himself when he was sick. Mom would have been right there holding my hand and telling me that I was going to be just fine. Giving any of us juice or crackers. Nope, you're not a nice person."

"Who asked you anyway, brat. Sit down and shut the hell up. If you're the one that I get, you can bet you'll be whipped daily. Even if I have to make up things about you to do it." Howard turned to the judge. "This here is the reason that I don't want any more females in my house. They're uppity and mouthy. Just listen to how she talks about me. I'd not hold her hand even if it had gold draped all over it."

"I wasn't talking about you. I was talking about my dad, Jeffery. He tells us he loves us every day. I wouldn't go with you even if the court lady there said we had to." The other two girls got up on their chairs too, and glared at him. "You're not a nice person at all."

Howard was applauded at their behavior. He didn't think that his wife was any happier about them either. Leaning in to ask her what she wanted to do, she said she didn't want them. That was perfect for him, and he smiled at the judge. Time to pack it in and get back home. He hated it here. There wasn't any place to smoke a good cigar or have a glass of good wine like he had at home, nor was he able to have meals brought to him every time he was hungry. A man like him was used to the finer things in life. He needed to have people waiting on him all the time.

"Your honor, ma'am, we've, my missus and me, we've decided that those kids are just too smart-mouthed for us. We'd like to withdraw our demands that Paige hand them over to us. She should have done a better job of raising them in the event I might want to have one of them someday. They have no respect for their betters, and I think they should be put in a military school just to make it so they learn some manners." He gave that a little more thought. "I'm thinking now that we need to send our boy off to one of them schools. He needs to grow some balls and learn how to toughen himself up. So, I'm sorry we took up your time in this, and we'll be heading home."

"Your honor, there are other matters that we'd like to have taken care of concerning Mr. and Mrs. Murry." Howard asked the Rigging guy or whatever his name was what he was talking about. "There is child support for the Griffin girls. As well as the other children that Mr. Murry has fathered. Mrs. Murry has had full knowledge of the other children, including the Griffin girls, that had her making sure that they were put into the worse situation they could have been in. Going so far as to have Mrs. Griffin—"

"Who the hell are you talking about?" The man told him it was his daughters as well as Paige Griffin. "I don't know a Paige Griffin. Her name is Paige Dasher. You should get your facts straight, sir."

"That's their new adoption name for the girls as well as Paige is married to my brother." He asked the judge if that was a conflict of difference. The other lawyer corrected him. "Whatever you want to call it. You should be on my side of the table, not over there seeing to the brats that Paige had. Have you listened to them talking to me? Bad raising if you ask me."

"Or it could be that you've made them so upset with your comments on their half-brother that they're justified in what they're saying." Howard told him that they weren't his kids if he wasn't claiming them. He handed him another file as well as the judge. "What is this? I'm not paying them child support, you idiot. They're not mine."

"It's been established, Mr. Murry, that the children are yours. And I'll decide what you're going to be paying these little girls and the others that you've left to their own devices." The judge looked over the paperwork and then asked the other guy for more information. He was a suck-up, was all Howard could think of calling him. But he kept his mouth shut. He was an abnormally large man to be messing with. "I'm going to call a recess for thirty minutes to look over this paperwork. Mr. and Mrs. Murry, you'll stay right here in this courtroom with a guard on you so that you don't skip out on what I'm thinking will be an awakening call for the two of you."

When the judge left the room, Howard decided that he'd had enough of this crap. He wanted to go home and wished he'd never stepped foot in this area. However, the moment that he stood up, the police were right there by him. He couldn't have taken a piss without one of them going with him, he was told. Even Rachel wasn't being let go. This was just stupid.

At least lunch was brought in for them. It wasn't anything that he would have gotten for himself, but he ate it. After being told there wouldn't be anything else, he decided that the turkey and ham was good enough. He thought that a nice big bag of chips, not the cheap kind, would have been good but he was told that it wasn't a healthy choice. Like he gave two shits about his health right now.

It was nearly right on the dot when the bailiff came back into the room. The judge was delayed. He noticed that the girls were gone now, and he was glad for that. Their mouthiness wasn't putting him in the best of mood. Before anything could be said about them getting out of there, he was called to the office of the judge, along with his wife and the other guy.

"Mr. and Mrs. Murry, I've just gotten word for you to go to the hospital for your son." Rachel asked what he'd done now. That she wasn't going to be babying him when she just wanted to get him home. "They said that they needed to talk to the two of you immediately that your son isn't well."

"Of course, he's not well. You were told that a bit ago by this guy. Again, what's he done now? I'm not paying for anything that those people did to him. I didn't say he could go, and it's not my bill." Rachel took the phone from the judge when it rang. She was hard on telling the person at the other end that she wasn't paying for shit. Then when she was quiet for a long time, he wanted to ask her what was going on. After the call, Rachel turned to him. "He's gone. Howie died an hour ago. They said that he had leukemia and that he'd not gotten proper care. How was I to know that when all he did was complain all the time." Rachel turned to the judge. "When can we get home? I have shit I have to do, and waiting around here for you to get your thumbs out of your ass isn't getting me any closer to doing them. I have two club meetings that I'm missing over this."

"Mrs. Murry, your son just passed away. Don't you want a minute to grieve for him?" Rachel told her that he'd been sickly for a while, and she wasn't going to miss any of that. "You really don't care that he's gone."

"No. I mean, I guess I'll miss having him around. He was a great way to break the ice when we'd go out, but he was a pain the way—well, I guess he really was ill, but he should have told me that he had leukemia. I mean, don't they let kids get tattooed with that sort of information now? It would certainly be helpful to know that. Howard, make a note on that. We'll petition for all kids to have their illnesses tattooed on them so that the parents will be aware of it."

The attorney sat down. Hard. His wife asked him what his issue was, and he only shook his head. Some people, like this guy, didn't understand how difficult it was to have a kid that was sickly all the time. He'd bet anything that the man was a homo too. There was just too much of that nonsense going on all the time nowadays, Howard thought.

"We're not finished here. Since you have so coldly decided that you're better off without your boy, we'll proceed. However, I want you both to understand that I'm not at all happy with your behavior. I can understand that people have different ways of grieving. But you two…you really are cold and heartless, aren't you?" Rachel said they were practical. "No, I have it right. Cold and heartless."

As they made their way to the courtroom again, he was struck by the difference a few minutes could make. People were glaring at them now. Not that they'd been all the nice before, but he had a feeling that, like the judge, they had been mislabeled. They weren't cold nor heartless. They were, as Rachel said, practical. Having Howie gone would make their lives less restrictive. It amazed him how many places wouldn't allow them to drop him off while they went out. It was, he thought, an outrage.

~*~

Jeffery was still sitting in the courtroom when his dad joined him. Looking at the man he loved with all his heart, he nodded when asked if he was all right. Dad told him that he looked less than all right, more like he'd seen a ghost.

"Their little boy died, and they had the nerve to ask us for child support. Why? I don't think I ever understood the reason they said." Dad told him what he'd heard. "So they thought that since Paige kept all the healthy genes for her daughters that it was somehow her fault that their little boy died? Dad, he didn't look good even before they came here for this."

"Some people, as we have come to realize, should never breed. Nor should they be allowed to have children when they do. That poor child. He'd been telling them for months—then they asked the judge to put it through that kids have their ailments written on them so that they'd remember. My goodness, Jeffery. I never heard of the likes before. Have you?" He told his dad that he'd not. "But they didn't get by with the things they'd done in the name of 'having money,' did they. That's going to be a nice nest egg for those beautiful girls when they get older. Even Judge Williams telling them that they had to pay the same amount to each of the other children was something I think they'd not expected."

"I don't think they either one expected to have to do anything that they didn't want to. I mean, the look on their faces when Judge Williams told them that their accounts were all sealed until they made restitution for the other families, was telling." Jeffery shook his head. "They never once seemed as if—I know that they said they didn't really care that Howie had passed, but they really didn't. He was just a kid."

"I've spoken to the doctor at the hospital. He said that he'd been very sick for a long time. By the time he'd made it to the hospital today, he'd already been past the point of helping him other than just giving him an easy passing. The little fella might have gone on to see his maker without a single thought that anyone ever loved him. I wish we had known about him sooner. I would have been with him to the end, so he wouldn't be alone. My heart hurts for him." Jeffery told his dad that the girls were hurting too. "I don't doubt that either, son. Those little girls they have big hearts. It wouldn't surprise me if they ask you if they can go to the funeral."

"They have, and we told them that we would. With their parents being in jail...I have to tell you, I was as surprised as Judge Williams was about some of the things that came out about them. To think that they'd been making it difficult on all the mothers of Howard's children for years is just not right on so many levels. Hopefully, this money coming to them will help a great deal. Paige wants to put it away for the girls. But they want nothing to do with it."

"I can see that as well. They're very opinionated, aren't they? I just love them to pieces, I tell you, son. I do. They say the darndest things those girls do. But when they say that they love you, it gets you right there in the feels so tightly that you surely feel like you could live in that and nothing else forever." Jeffery told his dad that he felt the same way when they called him dad. "Yes, I can hear that too. The first time that Edwin said it, durned near took me to my knees. Of course, I had to be all manly about it and not show how emotionally it got me. Oh, my son, you and your brothers are going to have a good time with all these kids coming around. I know that your mom and I are too. To have them come over and spend the day with us? Well, as I said, it gets us right in the feels. We're so looking forward to Christmas that you can't believe the lists that we have going right now."

Dad asked him if he'd like to have dinner with

him. The girls and Paige, too, of course. Mom had to go and see to something that she'd been putting off in favor of playing with the kids. When he asked Paige if she wanted to have dinner with his dad, she suggested he come to the house. They were having make-your-own pizzas tonight. Jeffery thought that his dad was going to beat him to his home. He was so excited to be doing that with the family than going out to dinner with them.

They walked to his home instead of calling for a limo. He told his dad about the talk that he'd had with the girls and how that had went over. Jeffery told him that he'd never had to say out loud how much money he'd been able to put away until that night. Then he told him about the nightmare that Amy had had about her biological father.

"Kids hear more than you think they do. I used to tell your mom that you boys had an extra set of ears for listening in on things that you shouldn't have had any knowledge of. But durned if you didn't know all about it." Jeffery laughed, telling his dad that they did know a great deal, but it was mostly Edwin that would tell them. "We figured that out a little too late, I'm thinking. It was that thing he could do with phones. But I don't know if he ever realized it or not, but he could do it with anything he put his mind to, like door knobs and the like. I saw him one time put his hand on a donkey and knew not just that the poor old thing was being abused but that who had done the abusing. He did right by the poor thing too."

His dad had never been a big fan of pizza. He used to tell them that it was just cheesy bread with red sauce over it. But when he started helping the girls out, he noticed that they were getting him to try things like black olives and hot peppers that none of them had ever been able to do before. His pizza was loaded up with as much stuff as his was, including dads all-time favorite, sliced tomatoes. He put a few on his own pizza just to not be outdone by his dad.

After a successful pizza-making event, Paige brought out the fixings to make banana splits. He noticed that his daughters were mostly eating the toppings of nuts and sprinkles and got a kick out of that. But his dad had made a large split by putting several bananas in a bowl, all cut up with all the toppings covering it. Then, of course, the required whipped cream topping. He and the girls ate out of his big bowl while watching television. Jeffery decided that it was past time to tell his new wife what he did for the government. But she surprised him once again and told him that she knew.

"Your sisters told me. And then your mom did." He told her that he wasn't aware that they knew about it. "Your entire family knows what you do, honey. They've known for a long time. They figured it out when you would lock yourself away for a few hours then they would read about it in the paper. You don't think you can get anything past your parents, do you?"

"I thought that I could." They both laughed. Dad told them to keep it down. They were enjoying the movie. *I know for a fact that my dad has seen this movie at least a dozen times. He and Mom have watched it at least once a month since it came out.*

Well, he's having a good time with the girls, and that's all I care about. When the movie was over, Dad helped him carry the girls up to bed. When they woke, asking for a story, it was his dad that read it to them. Jeffery remembered his dad doing the same thing with them when they were kids. It was a core memory that he'd share with his daughters soon.

Jeffery decided that he wanted to get together with his brothers and see what they could write up as stories for their children. Some of the memories that he had were too old to remember all the details, but he was sure that if they all got together, it would fill in the blanks.

Deciding that he wanted to spend more time with his family, his brothers, he was going to get them together one night and have a nice dinner out with them. That would be, he knew, a great way to bring up the stories that he wanted to put down on paper. Pictures too. He knew that he had several trunks of them in his upstairs that he was going to get out and share, too, not just with his kids but with anyone that wanted to share them.

As he was headed to his own bed that night, Jeffery felt better than he had in a good long time. He'd gotten things off his chest that he'd not known was bothering him. He'd had a great evening with his dad and children, and now he was going to sleep with his mate. While he didn't know what the night was going to bring to them, he was happy tonight just to be able to hold her.

As soon as he got into bed, thinking that Paige had already fallen asleep, she rolled over on top of him naked. It was all he could do not to come all over himself the way that she looked sitting atop of him.

"I've been stupid for not doing this sooner,

don't you think?" He nodded, then shook his head. "You're funny when you're aroused…I started to ask you if anyone had ever said that to you before, but I don't want to know."

"No one on this earth has ever had me aroused as much as you do right now." She giggled, a sound that he loved hearing from her. "Now, if you would be so kind as to slide over my full cock, I think that I can have a good deal of fun with—Christ woman, you're going to kill me."

She gave him a mischievous grin and said, "I thought it was time for us to have a little fun, don't you think?" She gave him a lingering kiss on the lips before straddling him between her legs. Jeffery felt his heart rate quicken as his arousal began to grow. He had yearned for this moment since he first set eyes on Paige. He wanted to savor it, and yet, the desire he felt was almost too much to contain.

"I think this is an excellent idea," He said, his voice raspy with need. Paige smiled and then leaned down, pressing her lips against his. He felt his whole body melt into the mattress as he kissed her back, savoring her sweet taste and the way she felt in his arms. He wanted to take this moment and make it last forever, but Paige had other ideas. She moved her lips away from his and began to trail kisses down his neck and chest, teasing him as she went.

Jeffery felt his body tense in anticipation as she moved lower and lower, her touches becoming more and more intimate. He closed his eyes, savoring the sensations that ran through his body and the way she made him feel. Finally, after what felt like an eternity, Paige reached her final destination. She took him in her mouth, exploring every inch of him with her tongue and lips. It was almost too much for him to take, and yet he didn't want it to end. He felt as though he could lay here forever, letting Paige drive him to the edge of pleasure over and over again.

Time seemed to stand still as Paige pleasured him, her technique becoming more and more skilled with each passing minute. Jeffery could feel the tension slowly building in his body, and when he finally reached his climax, it was almost too intense. He felt himself pulse and tremble as wave after wave of pleasure swept over him.

Jeffery flipped her over onto her back and suckled her right breast into his mouth. He teased the nipple with his tongue as his fingers dipped into her hot sheath. Paige gasped as Jeffery pleasured her, her hips bucking against his hand as she urged him on. Jeffery moved his lips further down her body, his tongue trailing a line of kisses along her abdomen. Paige moaned with anticipation as Jeffery slowly moved lower and lower, his tongue tracing a line over her thighs and legs. Jeffery turned his attention to her moist folds. Paige cried out his name as Jeffery's tongue ran over her. His soft lips teased her, causing her desire to burn out of control. She began to shudder as he pleasured her. Finally, she let out a cry as her body spasmed with pleasure, her orgasm washing over her like a tidal wave.

Paige was still reeling from her orgasm as Jeffery flipped her over onto her stomach and entered her from behind. He took her with long, deep thrusts, each one making her gasp with pleasure.

"Harder," She cried out, her words almost unintelligible.

Jeffery did as she asked, his body slamming into hers with a force that almost hurt. He loved the way he filled her up and the way she made him feel. He had never felt so whole before, and he never wanted it to end. He could feel her passion increasing, and he knew that she was nearing release. He increased his pace, hoping to drive her over the edge. When she cried out his name, he felt the release take him soaring to new heights as he came and then came again. Now too sated to hardly move. He rolled off Paige and drew her into his arms.

When he was finally able to catch his breath, Jeffery opened his eyes and looked up at Paige. He marveled at the beauty of her face, and as she smiled down at him, he knew that he was the luckiest man in the world.

Chapter 6

While Jeffery didn't want to be at the jail to talk to Howard and his wife, he was just in too good a mood to turn down the opportunity to talk to the man. When the call had come in this morning requesting that he go down to the jail, he'd nearly turned it down to spend the day with his little family. But since Paige and the girls were spending the day with his mom, he thought he'd be better off going there rather than hanging out with the rest of them. He'd not get into as much trouble, he thought.

He'd had to wait for a little while on the man. His wife had already shown up to the little room they were in, but she wasn't saying a word. That was fine by Jeffery. He didn't care for her any more than he did Howard. And he despised the man. When

Howard was brought in, he looked a little worse for wear. Laughing at the sight of him all roughed up and his lip bloodied, he didn't bother even asking him what had happened.

"I'm a busy man, Howard. What is it that you want with me?" He told him that he wanted out of jail. "I don't think that is going to happen anytime soon. It was my understanding that you're here with Rachel awaiting sentencing. Plus, I don't know what you think I would do to get you out. You threatened my family."

"They say you have a great deal of money. All of you Griffin people do. People up here get mighty testy when you bad mouth the hand that feeds them, don't they?" Rachel huffed, and Jeffery asked her what her issue was. "She's pissed off because she doesn't get to go home and tangle with a few people that testified against her."

"They have no right talking about me. I do what I do because I enjoy it. If they don't know how to behave, then someone, me, should be able to point it out to them without them getting pissed off and talking about me." Jeffery asked if that included treating her stepchildren that way. "Stepchildren? No, I'll never claim those brats. You can have them.

However, I've decided that if you want to keep them, you're going to pay out the ass for it. You're going to pay off some people so that we can get out of here. Or, and this is not a threat, young man, I'll make sure those little girls you're so proud of never make it to their next birthday. I have contacts that would surprise you. And kill you if I wish it."

"You're threatening me in a jail where you've been told that they record everything that you say and do. That's sort of ballsy, don't you think? Not to mention against the law. Aren't you in enough trouble as it is?" She told him that since she'd not authorized her being recorded, then they couldn't use it against her. "I'm afraid that it doesn't work that way. Once you're in jail, all your rights to privacy are out the window. In answer to your question, no, I'm not going to pay off people to get you out of here. I like you both right where you are. I know that my family sleeps better knowing that you're not running around terrorizing other children and their mothers. By the way, I heard the first little guy got his check this morning. Yay for him and his mom. You two aren't going to have shit when and if you ever get out of jail. Or prison, depending on what the judge wants to do with you two."

"That's just what I thought you'd say. Howard, tell him what we're going to do to him if he doesn't comply." Rachel looked at him. He saw something that he thought she never hid from her targets. Evilness. When Howard didn't speak, they both turned to look at him. "What is wrong with you? I told you to tell him what our plans were."

"In the event, you didn't hear me, Rachel, love. I told him. He turned us down. I don't know what else you want me to say." She told him to tell him again. Howard turned to him. "If you don't help us get out of here, we're going to make it so that the little girls you love so much don't make it to their next birthday. And Rachel has contacts all over the place. She really does too. I think she has eyes in the back of her head too. I'm just finding out—ouch. What the fuck was that about? Why did you hit me?"

"You make me sound like a tyrant. I'm far from that. I'm just a good citizen that likes to have things done the way that I want them. And if I don't, then I make people do it that way. Christ, why did I ever marry you." She pretended to think about it. Or she had to. Jeffery didn't know. But he was enjoying the show. "Oh, I married you because my father made me because you knocked me up with that worthless brat that went and died on us. You have no idea how much I'm going to miss his usefulness."

"That's enough." Jeffery stood up but sat down when he thought of something that he wanted to say to these people. "I wouldn't help you with anything. Not only that but even if my life depended on it, I'd still walk away. And you won't be able to kill any of my family, my daughters included, because we're immortal. You'll also learn that I can be just as mean and a tyrant as the two of you are. More so, I'm betting."

He put his hand on the table, and without taking his eyes off the two people sitting there, he let his wolf show through. Digging his claws deep into the table, when his hand morphed into his paw, he knew he'd be asked to replace it as soon as he left.

Rachel pulled his paw from the table and laid it against her cheek. It was the sickest thing he's ever had done to him. Jerking his hand away from her, he scratched her. When she took her blood to her mouth and moaned, Jeffery stood up and had to count to ten before he could move to the door to leave the two of them.

As soon as he was out the door, Jeffery leaned against the opposite wall and slid to the floor. His wolf was curled around him, but he wasn't sure if it was comfort for him or his beast. Putting his head on his knees, he heard someone coming toward him and didn't bother looking up. He knew who it was, and he wasn't sure what to say to her.

"You all right?" He told Storm to go away. "I can't. I can feel your pain, and it's hurting me. Edwin is on the floor at home in pain because yours is so profound. I think that the only reason that I was able to get up and move is because my wolf needed to be near you to feel better. Tell me you're all right?"

Instead of telling her what would be a lie, he told her what had happened. Leaving nothing out. Jeffery finally raised his head and looked at her. He could see her own pain and told her that he was sorry.

"I'm going to kill them both." Jeffery told her not to do it. That they needed to serve their time. "If they don't, then I'm going to kill them both. Long and without mercy. Not just for what they've done to you today but for those nieces of mine too. I heard about Amy's nightmare. He did that to her. Did she tell you that? That he threatened her with taking her from her sisters one afternoon?"

"She didn't tell me that, no. Does her mom

know?" Storm said that she didn't and thought that it would be better coming from him and Amy. Jeffery stared at the door. He knew that they were no longer in the room. The jailer would have carted their asses away when he left, but the thought of them trying to take his daughter was almost more than he could take right now. "I want them both dead. But I'm not going to do it, nor are you. I don't want you to have to tell my daughters what you did. And you would if they asked."

"I would. It's no less than they deserve is to know that he's paid. And trust me, Jeffery, he will. Both of them will have paid the price when I'm finished with them." Of that, he had no doubt. But he didn't want her to do it. "Then who? Rain? I think that she'd be worse on them than I would be. There is no one else."

"There is. The pack." Storm sat down beside him now and leaned against the wall. "Those two hurt a member of Edwin's pack. Not only that, but they threatened his brother too. Not just me but Edwin himself while in the courtroom as they were being taken out. It wouldn't be quick with them. It would be bloody and painful too. Being dead is good enough for me so long as someone tells them what it is that they've been killed for."

"Edwin would gladly do this for you. I mean, have the pack do it." Jeffery thought that he would as well. "I can't get out of my mind that they hurt him because of your pain. I've never seen him so hurt for anyone before."

"We're all connected that way. I bet if you were to ask, my parents felt it as well as the mother of the earth. We all have a connection with everything." She nodded. "You're telling him what happened, aren't you?"

"He asked. And yes, he said that he'd do it. Gladly. He said that he'll take care of it, that for you to not say a word to anyone. Well, Paige but no one else." He said he'd not. But if his daughters were to ask, he'd tell them too. "You think they will? Ask, I mean?"

"Yes. A pack of wolves takes out their worst nightmares? Yes, they'll ask." He thought about Amy's face when she'd been scared of a dream—a reality that had happened to her. "No, they won't ask now that I think about it. They'll just know. When they turn up dead by any means, I think they'll know that someone in this family took care of them for them. And I'm betting that they never say a word to anyone but each other."

"You're probably right." The longer they sat there, just the two of them, the more Jeffery realized that he was right. "I've spoken to your brother, and everything is set. Don't ask. He said that he'll tell you that he heard from the station house, and that's all that will be said about it."

"I can do that." He took her out to lunch. Once his belly was feeling better, he knew that he'd be able to hold things down. It had made him that ill to have had Rachel doing that to him. Shivering once more, he ordered himself a large taco salad and decided that was all he needed for a meal in the middle of the day. Actually, it was the women in his life that were changing his eating habits, and he couldn't find anything wrong with it.

Taking her home since he'd driven to the station, he wasn't surprised to find a few cars that he didn't know in his brother's drive. He asked Storm about it and she laughed. He had to smile. He loved the women in his family.

"They're the newest pack leaders around the country. They're here because Edwin put it out there that he was going to be making new laws and making people adhere to them." He asked if they were upset with them. "No. They're terrified that if they don't follow them correctly, then he's going to come down on their asses. Or ask Rain or I to do it for him. We have a good reputation around for getting things settled."

They both laughed, and he had to hand it to his big brother. He was good, but his wife and sister-in-law were scary as fuck. He knew that they scared all of his brothers just enough that they never wanted to cross them. Jeffery also thought that a person would have to be stupid not to be a little afraid of the women in their family, including his daughters.

~*~

Jeffery decided that he was going to grill out tonight for his family. Since the cook was off today, he loved being able to mess around in the kitchen. So long as he didn't have to do it daily, he thought that in times like this, he'd be all right. Jeffery did have a couple of normal jobs to do in the morning, but for now, he was all right with not answering his phone unless he had to. As soon as Amy and the other two came into the kitchen with him, he knew that something was wrong. Asking them about it, it was Glory that huffed at him.

"There doesn't have to be anything wrong,

you know. We're just frustrated with how things are going after school." Setting up the potatoes for salad, he casually asked her what had frustrated her. She shrugged again but talked to him too. "It wasn't at school but on the way home. There was this kid, a little girl that was standing by one of the street signs by the Millers Emporium. What is an emporium anyway?"

"It usually means a large store that is selling a lot of different things. But since I know that the Miller store just sells meats and cheeses, I guess that could count too." She nodded, and he watched as Amy made a note in her little book she'd been carrying around. "What was the little girl doing? I mean, she was with someone, right?"

"No. She was tied to the sign. Like she was this dog or something." Glory asked him how to spell emporium, so he told her and then asked her what she meant. He noticed that all three of them had different notebooks they wrote things in. "She was tied up. With this rope, a bright orange one so you couldn't miss it, wrapped around her arms. Her wrists, I guess. Why would someone do that?"

"Did you tell the driver?" He said that he'd go back there when he dropped us off. But Amy made a fuss, and he did it with us in the car. She didn't look good, so he said he'd call the police."

"Where is he now?" Libby said that he was still in the driveway when they came in. "All right. Let's go and see what we can find out. I'm like you. I don't like the thought that she was being treated like a dog."

"Yeah, I hoped you'd say that." He went to the door, and the driver was still there. He had a small child on his lap, and so many things rushed through his head in that moment. Things that could get the young man into trouble with the police. It was Libby this time who ran up to the little girl. He knew before getting too close, he knew that the child was a wolf. He spoke to his brother.

"Blond kid with the bluest eyes you've ever seen?" He told Edwin that she could be his girl's sister. "I don't know that she is or not, but her parents were killed about six months ago. Car accident, if I remember. But the little girl, Rose, has been staying with her granny. Not wolf. You don't think that she's treating her like that because of what her dad was, do you?"

"I haven't any idea. But Libby and the other two are talking to her. Toby, our driver, picked the girl up when she was at the store. He didn't go in, but this could be bad if she says that he kidnapped her." Edwin said he was on his way with Stone. "All right. We're out front. But I'm going to invite them inside so that she can get warm. The little thing doesn't even have on boots but sandals that look a little too small for her."

After getting the child in the house, he felt better for it. It was cold out, not freezing, but he did worry with her having inappropriate shoes on. After getting her a snack with his daughter, Toby was sent on his way. He also told him not to say a word about what he'd done. While Jeffery wasn't sure what would come around about him taking the child, he didn't want to cause trouble if he didn't have to.

Rose was more hungry than a few slices of apples could have filled her. As soon as Paige came home, she made the four girls some chocolate milk and gave them a few cookies. She told him she'd heard about the little girl and had gone to the store to find her. Toby was just leaving when she noticed that she was gone.

"Her granny has been complaining about having to raise an animal since her son died. He was driving but has been trying to say that the daughter-in-law was. Causing an uproar with the woman's family too." He asked her where she'd heard that. "Your mom. She knows everything and everyone, I guess."

"She does. I think that I'm only just realizing how far reaching she is. Dad, too but Mom is better. So what do you want to do with her?" She asked him what he meant. "She's treating the child like an animal. You heard that she's upset to be raising her. I'm thinking that by the end of the day, we're going to have four daughters and not three."

"Would that bother you? To take in another child that isn't your own." He said it wouldn't if it didn't bother her. He'd take all the kids in that were being hurt like this if he could. "Good. I've already spoken to Rain. She's getting the information that is needed to make sure that we get her if the grandmother shows her true colors."

Smiling at Paige, he went to check on the girls. The television was on, but none of them were watching it. His daughters were comforting Rose. She was telling them about how her granny makes her sleep in a cage, and she gets hosed down once a day. That was all it took for him to tell his brother that granny wasn't getting the little girl back.

"All right. I'm nearly to the police station. Believe it or not, when I called the station, they said that granny, her name is Beatrice Cody, had left the store and was home when they went to check up on her. I have a feeling that is why the child was put outside. So that someone would come along and take her. That's grounds for child abuse. Not to mention the things that you told me about." He asked what the police thought. "I'm on my way inside now. Can you not clean the child up. I hate to ask you that because I know that Paige is more than likely looking for something for her to wear right now but don't do it. All of you come to the station now and tell them, minus Toby's part, what happened. I don't know how you're going to swing that, but just try not to get him into trouble. He's only nineteen and working for college money. All right?"

"I'll make sure the girls know too." He put things away in the kitchen and was barely able to get any of the four women in his household to not clean up little Rose. The child was filthy and smelled bad, but right now, he wanted to get this ended so that she'd be able to live in a judgment-free home. And a loving one too.

They were at the police station by the time Mrs.

Cody had been brought in. As soon as she saw Rose, she came at her with her hand up to no doubt smack her. Before either he or Paige could react, it was Libby that stood in front of Rose.

"You touch her again, and I will break your fingers off and stick them down your throat. You want to pick on someone. You just mess with me." He didn't move, nor did the grandmother. Rose wrapped her arms around Paige's leg when the elderly woman looked at the child. "I'm not kidding you, lady. You back away from her right now. My momma won't be able to save you if you don't."

"Just what I thought. A bunch of bratty children that are dogs, no doubt like this one is." Libby lifted her chin up and told her that at least they weren't monsters. "You think that's what I am? I have news for you. Had I been at the scene of the accident when she killed my little boy, then none of them would have survived."

"That's enough." Libby and his other two daughters took Rose's hand and walked her away from the adults. Paige asked Mrs. Cody if she really would have killed the child. "I mean, you've had her for six months or so now. How has she lived this long if that was your plan."

"It's not for lack of trying." She eyed Edwin when he stood up. "Oh, don't try your dog shit on me. I know what you are. I know that you're old and crap. I don't care. Take her. For all I care about her, she can live with the dogs like the rest of you."

"You're a piece of work, aren't you, Mrs. Cody?" He'd not known that his mom and dad had joined them. Dad took Mom's hand into his and kissed the back of it before turning back to Mrs. Cody. "I've known you for your whole life, and you're no different now than you were all those years ago when Herbert Johnston turned you down when you asked him to the dance that year you turned eighteen. I'm thinking that's where you got your bitterness from about our kind. He turned you down, with good reason, I've come to understand, and you just couldn't handle that. Well, I'm here to tell you that you're going to be fined by the pack for your treatment of this child. I told you that when you took her in that the pack would be providing for her, and you said that was all right. There were rules you had to follow. I'm sure you remember us going over them with you."

"She's part of the reason that I lost my son. Every time I look at her, I see him there. Those blue eyes on that thing. I never spent a dime on that kid. You can have every penny of it back. I don't want her either. She's a nasty reminder that I've lost it all." Paige told her that she'd not lost her grandchild. "She's not mine. Never will I call it that, either. Christ, good riddens. You have no idea how thrilled I was when she was gone when I came out of Millers. Then the police showed up, and I thought good lord, someone has thankfully killed it so that it couldn't breed more like it. Well, take it. I want nothing to do with it."

Mrs. Cody didn't even put up a fuss when she was arrested, either. Taking the money out of her handbag, she threw it at his parents. Child endangerment carried a hefty fine around here. Jeffery was sick of seeing it too. When they were able to take Rose to the hospital to make sure that she'd not been harmed much more, Jeffery made his way home with the girls. They wanted to have Rain come over so that they could get a room ready for their new sister, and they also asked for a shared room.

"Shared room? I mean, I think I understand what that means, but you tell me." They did in great excitement and detail. "I like that. And since we haven't put televisions in your rooms, this will make a great way for the four of you to be able to watch it together."

They were so excited when they got home, and Rain was there. After she asked him what he wanted her to do, Jeffery was happy to tell her to do what the girls wanted. She was smiling when she went up to the bedrooms with the girls. And when Paige came home with a cleaned-up Rose, he almost didn't recognize her. He thought it might have had a lot to do with the huge smile on her face more than anything.

Dinner that night was a great deal of laughter around the table. Rose joined right in with the girls like she'd been around them her entire life. He had a feeling that it was going to be like that with anyone the girls met. They'd be instant friends. However, he also thought that if someone made an enemy of even just one of them, that would be it. They'd have an enemy of all four of them. That's just the way they rolled, as his dad was so fond of saying.

"I feel like this was meant to be." He asked Paige what she meant. "Well, we couldn't save Howie because we didn't get a chance to be there for him. But we were able to do that for this little girl."

"I think I might have to agree with you." She

asked him if he was finished taking in little girls. "Never. I love all the women in my household. They scare me a bit, too, but I'd not trade anything for them. They're all mine. That would include you too."

They went by the shared room to have a look around and found all four of the girls asleep on the floor. They'd gotten sleeping bags, too, that were so bright pink that the moon was the only thing that was brighter. Kissing the four of them on the head, he was happy with the way things turned out. And as he'd said to Paige, he'd have it no other way.

Chapter 7

Paige had had enough of waiting around to have sex with Jeffery again. Now that they were in bed together, no one was calling, or there weren't any late-night things going on, she decided that she was going to get laid or kill him. This was so much better. The first time they'd had sex, it had been quick. She wanted so much more this time, and she was going to get it.

His hands were rough, and she loved the way that they felt when he touched the most tender part of her body. Her nipples, her hips. When he asked her about a scar that she had on her right leg, she had to make her mind work so that she could remember.

"I fell. Yes, that feels wonderful." Pacing herself, she tried to think what she had been saying.

"I was pregnant with the girls. I'd just found out that morning that I was having triplets, and I had thoughts of giving them away for adoption. I thought that there wasn't any way that I'd be able to raise one, much less three of them at the same time."

He rolled her to her back. Wrapping her legs around his hips, she couldn't believe how much better this was. To have him so deep inside of her that she could have sworn that he was touching the back of her throat. Jeffery stopped moving and told her to finish."

"Finish?" He laughed and told her about the scar. "Yes, the—now? You want the story now? All right. It was early spring, but there had been an overnight freeze. I slipped on the icy sidewalk and realized just as I was going down that I was going to harm them. Rolling to my back, I protected them with my arms, and I hit my leg on one of the fire hydrants right outside the clinic I had just left. It was a deep bruise that had me laid up for a few weeks. But it was the children that I was most worried about. When I was rushed to the hospital, I started to bleed a little."

He wiped the tears that had fallen while thinking about what had happened. Jeffery told her how much he loved her and was glad that things had turned out all right. When she nodded, Paige knew that she had to tell him the rest of the story.

"They told me that I might lose them. All or one, they didn't know at that point. But I told them that I needed them. I wanted them. It was at that moment that I knew that if I lost them, I'd die myself. They were going to be my world, and I'd do anything to stop them from being harmed again. I felt like I'd caused myself to hurt them, and it took me a long time to get over that feeling." He told her that he loved her and she looked at him. "You're my heart, Jeffery. Every part of my life has been working up to finding you and having you in my life. I know that I resisted at first, not that anyone could blame me, but once I let you into my heart and life, I couldn't imagine a life without you and our daughters."

He kissed her, and she put all her love into kissing him back. When he made love to her again, she knew she'd never love anyone else, but this man and she was glad for it. As he pulled her hands up and over her head, she held onto the headboard as he made his way down her body. His cock left her bereft for only a few moments, but as soon as he took her breast, all of it, into his mouth, she cried out in so much pleasure that she worried that the girls would hear her.

But as he moved down her body to her navel, she didn't care if the world heard her. She was going to enjoy this even if it incapacitated her for the rest of her life. This was her night, and she needed it as much as he did.

He lapped at her navel, bringing her so much pleasure that she doubted that she'd ever be the same after this. When he moved down lower, at her hips, then her pussy, she tensed up. When he took her clit into his mouth and nibbled gently, she came screaming out his name so loudly that she knew that she'd be having a sore throat in the morning.

He ate at her pussy until she was worn out from coming so many times. Each time that she thought she couldn't take anymore, he'd move in a way that would have her not feeling like she was getting enough of him.

His fingers and his tongue were inside of her, touching off parts of her that she'd never felt before. When she came again, her legs wrapped around his neck, she felt his fingers pull her gently from his neck, and she came again. Christ, she thought, this was better than anything in the world.

When she simply couldn't wait any longer for him to fuck her, she pulled his head up from her. Just looking at him, seeing him staring at her with a drugged look on his face, her juices dripping from his chin, made her come again.

When he moved up her body, kissing and nipping at her flesh, she begged him to take her. As soon as he slammed his cock into her, she passed out for a few seconds as her body came apart with the most epic climax she'd ever had.

"Come again, love. I need to feel you come like that again." She told him that she couldn't. That it was too much. But when he told her, commanded her to come, she bowed up from the bed, holding onto Jeffery as she came even harder than she had the last time. She felt the moment that he released.

He filled her with hot cum. Her own body, still reeling from coming so hard, tried to catch up to him, but there was no stopping him from coming a second time. When he bit down on her throat, she knew that he'd drawn blood. Paige came again but passed out before she could enjoy the completeness of it.

She woke with Jeffery holding her. When she asked him if he was all right, he laughed. Thinking about smacking him, she didn't have the strength to even lift her hand up, much less use any energy to do him harm. When he pulled her into his arms, Paige figured that she could forgive him of just about anything right now. Then her body started to tingle.

"Jeffery?" That's all she was able to get out when her body felt as if it was being turned inside out. Everywhere on her body, she could feel something like bugs crawling over her. Reaching for Jeffery, she realized that he was in pain too. And whatever was happening to her was happening to him as well.

Thinking that at some point she'd passed out, Paige reached for Jeffery. He was sitting in the chair by the bed, looking out the window. Sitting up took too much effort, so she just said his name softly. When he smiled at her, she knew that everything was going to be all right.

"We've bonded." She told him she'd figured that out when they had sex again. "Yes, well, what I mean is, you and I have more magic. A great deal of it too. By the way, I checked on the girls. They're still sound asleep."

"I remember thinking at some point they'd hear us." He said that his magic had sealed off the room when they needed to be not heard. "But not all the time. You did hear Amy crying."

"You will be able to now as well. You're not a wolf, but you have all the magic of one. The girls, all four of them, will also have magic." Paige asked him how he knew that. "I've been talking to Storm and Rain. They said they can almost taste how strong the two of us are. Storm told me, too, that it was to protect the children that come into our lives. I asked her what she meant by that, and she told me that you and I were going to be a safe haven for children like Rose. Also, before I forget, she's had her paperwork pushed through, and she's our daughter with our last name."

"You know, I just realized that I know nothing about her. How old she is or anything like that." He told her what Storm had been able to find out. "So she's five. Not too much difference in ages between them. And wolf. I think I might have known that from what Mrs. Cody was saying." She laughed.

"She is a wolf, an alpha's daughter. Her mom, Roslyn, was born to an alpha too, that took his own life when his granddaughter was given to Mrs. Cody. He took his daughter's death very hard as he'd only recently lost his wife to an accident a few weeks earlier." She asked him why Mrs. Cody got her, then. "I'm working on that now. I think that she thought that the child wasn't a wolf. It happens at times."

He crawled into bed with her, and she snuggled up to his warm body. Jeffery told her of the things that he knew that the two of them would share and why he thought that they were going to be a haven.

"It's this house. It was magical when we built it hundreds of years ago. We, even then, were taking care of people that stayed here. But now it's even more magical so that, as I said, we can keep children or whoever needs us to keep them out of harm's way will be safe here." She told him that was a wonderful thing. "I thought you'd say that. Now, here is what made it happen like it did. We would have gotten the magic anyway, but in smaller doses. But we're going to be called first when there is a child harmed that is brought into the hospital. A safe haven, as I said. We might not adopt all of them that come here, but we will love them and provide for them."

"Why do I have the feeling that there is a child now that needs us." He laughed and told her not that he was aware of. "But it could be soon. Are we going to be ready for that?"

"We are. Rain gave me a list of things that we'd need to have as supplies around here. Mostly it's diapers, and we'll have faeries around all the time.

Not just for the extra hands to help out but to also get things that we might need in a hurry for them. Beds and stuff like that." She told him that she could understand that. "Good. There is more, but nothing that we have to deal with tonight. The kids will be up in a couple of hours, and we need to get some rest. I have a job too in the morning, a regular one, and I need to be up for it. The police station is going to be putting in cameras in each cell to make sure that nothing is going on."

"Something happen?" He told her no, but that didn't mean that it wouldn't. "Good. I'm exhausted. And if we have sex like that again, I might need to be hooked up to an IV with some kind of energy drug in it to be able to move again." They both laughed.

"You'll need to eat more red meat. So will the girls. And to drink juice." When he yawned a second time in as many minutes, she put her head on his chest and listened to his heart beating. It was the most relaxing thing she'd ever heard. Closing her eyes, she fell to sleep immediately.

Waking up, she looked over to find Rose standing by the bed. When she asked her if she was all right, she nodded and then shook her head. She'd wet her bed. Getting up and dressing herself quickly, she made her way down the hall to get her cleaned up, all the while telling her that it was all right.

"I woke up and was scared, Ms. Griffin." She told her that she could call her Paige or whatever if she wanted. "If it's all right, can I call you mom like the others do? I'll not embarrass you about it."

"I promise you that I will never be embarrassed to have you call me mom." After giving her a quick shower and clean clothing, she got rid of the bedding in the laundry room and put her to bed with Libby when she opened her sleeping bag. Rose got in with her and told her new sister that she was sorry.

"You don't have to be. It happens. You've been having a lot of things going on today. We're all good." They snuggled down in the bed, and that was when Paige noticed that the bag they were in had enlarged to accommodate the two of them. Amy and Glory moved their sleeping bags closer to Rose and Libby and settled down.

Paige watched them as they fell asleep again. Rose looked at her before she closed her eyes and blew her a kiss. Paige felt as if she'd actually touched the child with her lips. The kiss had meant so much to her. Turning off the overhead light, she made her way to the kitchen when she realized that the sun was coming up. She wasn't the least bit surprised to find not only Edwin there but Jeffery too.

"I was just talking to Jeffery about what will be coming to you two for taking in Rose. While I know that you don't need it, it will go a long way in making her future better because she'll be cared for by the pack too." She asked him if it was necessary or could another family use it. "Yes, it's necessary. And it's going to be helpful when Mrs. Cody is brought up before the pack. She said she didn't spend the money, but she had. A great deal of it. The money that was collected at the station was all there was left. She had been using the money to try and get someone to kill off the little girl."

"Can I kill her?" Edwin said that the police were handling it. "All right, but if they don't, I will."

"Duly noted. Also, Howard and Rachel are dead. Don't ask me what happened, but since they threatened myself and Jeffery as well as you when they tried to take the girls, they were dealt with by the pack." She asked him if they had suffered. "I'm sure not as much as you'd like for them to, but they're gone. You can tell the girls whatever you want, but I'd like to suggest you tell them the truth. They'll find out if you don't."

"I think that they'll know anyway, don't you?" Edwin said that they would. Or they'd make their own decisions about how it had happened, and that might be bad too. "I agree. We'll tell them in the morning."

After Edwin left then Jeffery, she sat in the kitchen thinking about the events that had led up to where she was today. She had four daughters, a husband and a home. Nothing, not even her little girls when she'd met Howard. He'd been, she had thought at the time, the dream man that she'd been waiting for. Boy, did that turn out to be wrong.

When the girls joined her, she made them cereal. Normally she didn't care for the sweet stuff, but they'd all had a rough few days. When they were finished up, she sent them to take showers and get dressed. Paige did the same. Today was for them, she thought and was going to enjoy being out and about and not stressed.

Chapter 8

"Dad, when we were talking to Mrs. Cody, what did you mean when you said that her being turned down was well deserved?" Dad laughed, and it made Jeffery want to know what had happened all the more. "I'm going to love this story, aren't I?"

"I believe you might." Dad leaned back on the rocker that he'd taken to using after supper when they were all over. There were two more chairs like his father's, homemade by him in the winter months to keep him from getting on mom's last nerves. "Beatrice wasn't a beauty. I don't know that many people thought that she was even pretty. She was big, not fat but big like a man. Her hands too. They were about as large as mine were when I would shake hands with her. And my oh my, she had a grip too.

Like she was going to squeeze the life out of any part of you that she touched. But that wasn't what made her deserving of not having a date for the dance that year."

Dad looked at the evening tree line and smiled again as he remembered. Jeffery had a feeling that his father was there again. And when he began talking again, Jeffery could see the events as they happened that fateful day. He smiled, knowing that his dad was going to enjoy the telling of this story as much as he was going to hearing it.

"Bea, what everyone called her back then, had turned eighteen the day before this big dance that was at the old high school. She'd been primping for a few weeks. I guess you could call it experimenting with makeup and the like. Her daddy raised her all on his own, with her having four older brothers. I think, while I'm not sure, but I think that's what contributed to her manly ways." Dad laughed. "I don't mean to be a bastard about her looks. I guess some might have called her all right. But she was as homely as an old dog about to be put out to pasture. She wore her brother's castoffs too. Jeans and whatnot. And she was out there working with them with the cattle they raised back then too. My the memories that this brings up."

Dad was quiet for a few minutes, and Jeffery was all right with that. Something that he'd learned about his father, he had to have all his facts in a row before he would tell you something. He thought that was where Stone got it from. Facts Dad always had told them was the difference between being right or wrong about something. When he began again, Jeffery listened.

"Herbert Johnston. He was a big boy. At fifteen, he was bigger than his daddy and heavier than most of the cattle his family raised for eating. Not so many as the Handles had, Bea's maiden name, but they would share if they had enough to feed their family. But mostly to other shifters. He was a wolf too." Dad smiled. "Herbert looked so much like Bea that people were hard-pressed to remember that they weren't related. As I said, Bea was sort of manly. Anyhow, Bea makes her way to the pack land. Huffing and puffing each hard step of the way. There was a dust cloud that came up behind her that people thought afterwards should have been a forewarning of things to become. I was working with Herbert and his daddy when she came to find him."

"Mr. Johnston, Mr. Griffin. I'd like a word with

your son, please." Dad told him that he'd had to look around, not understanding why she'd want to speak to his boys by coming all the way out to pack land. But she cleared it up, he said, that she'd wanted to talk to Herbert. "He and I have some business to attend to."

"Business?" Dad said that was just what she called it. Business, not a date. Jeffery laughed. "So she thought that she'd approach it in a business manner? Sounds about right for her. What did Herbert say?"

"Now, don't you be getting ahead of my story, son." He smiled bigger. "She was all hot and sweaty, Bea was. Her hair might have been in some kind of braid, but by the time she'd footed it out where we were working, a good four miles, it looked like she'd stuck her fingers in a socket or something. Cheeks were all red, and her dress, and I swear she had on her oldest brother's boots, were all dusty and dirty. But there she stood, hands on her hips and her booted foot tapping away. Don't to this day know what she expected us to do. We were hands-deep in helping a cow birth her baby. Couldn't just walk away from that.

"Well, now, she decided, I guess, that we weren't going to leave, and she turned to Herbert.

He was a big man, like I said, but he was about as shy as—you surely remember him, don't you, son? He worked for the grocery store until he was about fifty. Never married or dated so far as I remember. I think he went to his grave as a virgin. Couldn't even summon up the words to tell his daddy that he'd been hurt one day and he died from a staph infection. Simple little splitter in his big toe took his life." Dad seemed to mourn the passing of the man, and it hurt Jeffery to know that his father had lost a friend, perhaps. "He just stared at Bea, and when she summed up her own courage to ask him something, his daddy and I were both privy to it all."

Dad rocked for a few minutes, then sat back up. There was a pain in his face. Wishing that he'd not asked his dad about it made him feel guilty for putting that pain there. But his dad told him that it was worth telling after all, and he wanted to have a good laugh with his son. So Dad continued.

"Herbert, you're going to be taking me to the dance tomorrow night. My daddy said you can even drive our car if you want. It's a fer piece to walk with me having on heels and the like." He just stared at her. Open mouth like he just couldn't believe that she was here, much less asking him out. "Are you stupid? I just told you that we're going to go to the dance. When you want to pick me up?"

"You're too heavy for me to pick up." She had looked at his daddy, and I then back at Herbert. "I don't know how to drive either, so I'm not going to take the car. You can't be wanting to go out with me either."

"Yes, I do. I have it all fixed up. And I can drive. So long as you don't tell my daddy I did it. And if you don't, then I'll give you a kiss at the end of the date. When you going to pick me up?" Herbert told her again that she was too heavy to be carting around. "Herbert, you aren't going to carry me. I'll have a car that you can take me in."

"I don't want to go on no date with you, Bea. People will talk about us." She told him right out that people were talking about her anyway. "Yes, I heard about all that stuff with Mr. Potter. I ain't going nowhere with you. You is spoilt."

"I tell you, son, I thought that she was going to go on asking him, but then something clicked in her head or something, and she picked up that big old machete that had been hanging in the barn and held it up above her head." Jeffery stopped rocking, and his heart started pounding. "We all thought for sure she was going to be chopping us all up before that calf was born. But all she did was pitch it toward the wall, you see. Stuck in the siding of the barn like a little bitty knife would in the ground. It quivering like it did, just vibrating like it was hooked up to something, scared me about to death, I tell you."

"I think I might have been terrified enough to take off running." Dad nodded but didn't speak for a few seconds. Then laughed. "You have to tell me how it ended."

"Herbert, as kind as any little puppy can be when someone is paying attention to it, walked over to the wall and took it out of the siding. Then, just as quick as a wink, he tossed the knife at Bea. Thought for sure it was going to hit her, but it landed between her dirty boots and stuck there. It was vibrating faster than it had when she'd tossed it, I tell you." Smiling, he told him the rest of the story. "Herbert's daddy and I backed up, leaving the cow to her own, when Bea pulled that knife out of the dirt and held it there. It was a waiting game, like two opposing monsters just waiting for the que to begin the fight again. But Herbert, he tells her that he's got no desire to date her. He called her spoilt again and told her to get on back to her house and reflect — that's just what he said, for her to reflect on her actions. Well, now, she took that big old knife with her and just as she was leaving the barn, she turned back to Herbert and told him that he'd better be picking her up at her house, or she'd make him sorry."

"Did he pick her up?" Dad told him that he'd not. That Herbert had gone frog hunting with his other brothers, and there was never a word said about it again. "I don't understand. How is that what turned her against our kind?"

"Well, now, I didn't say that was the end of it, now did I?" Jeffery shook his head. "About a week later, no more than that, I don't believe, Bea turns up married to Mr. Cody. The poor man looked like he'd been beaten up prior to the ceremony. And there Bea was in her finery telling everybody that would listen that a wolf had knocked her up. That was the only reason that she'd married her new husband. She, of course, blamed it on Herbert." Dad laughed.

"Then there came the biggest commotion you ever heard when they were having the dance at the wedding. About fifty of the pack came in the big barn as their wolves and tore the place up." Dad laughed hard. "They didn't take too kindly of her telling everyone that she'd been knocked up by Herbert.

When just about everyone there was a wolf that was doing the serving, word got out how she was lying to everyone. The pack, they chased her all the way to her daddy's house, nipping and biting at her big old backside."

Jeffery laughed. He'd known that without Herbert and Bea being mates, that there was no way that she was carrying his child. Most of the town knew the story about Mr. Potter and Bea as well. Bea, it seemed, had been giving away her wears, as Dad called them, since she'd been about thirteen. No one believed that either Herbert or the poor man Mr. Cody was the father of the child. But Dad told him that was a story for another time.

~*~

Harmon held onto the little baby boy as he fed it its's bottle. He'd been doing research on newborn human babies for the last two months and was glad that he was going to be able to leave here soon. Not that he didn't like what he was doing. Volunteering at the nursery five days a week was fun. But he did not care for the gossip and shit that was going on between the three nurses that he had to work with. None of them were in this job for anything but to gather information to talk about the mothers that were here.

He didn't even bother looking up when one of the nurses started talking to him about the parents of the child he was feeding. Harmon rarely even bothered to say a word to them unless it was related to the children. It had been three weeks, and they still hadn't figured out that he didn't care for their way of working.

"The father has been out of work for nearly a decade, but that doesn't stop them from having baby after baby, does it? Stupid people." Beth was wrong about her information. Harmon knew for a fact that the father was working, and he had been for the supposed decade she claimed he wasn't. "If I were in charge, I'd cut off welfare help to these kinds of people so that they're not just breeding more children to get a higher return on their taxes."

"How do you suppose they're getting a return on their taxes if they're not working?" The second nurse, Winny, said. "I make good money, but I get shit back. Yet children of these kinds of parents are getting big tax refunds as well as welfare help. Probably even pay for their popping this kid."

"I think I've heard about enough." He'd not even noticed the head nurse standing behind him. The nurses said that they'd only been speculating on things. "You're being a bitch, the two of you, and I've had enough complaints about the two of you and Carol to last several lifetimes. What do you know of these people that makes you such an expert on their lives? Nothing, I'll tell you. Nothing at all. Now get to work and keep your mouths shut."

When Mable was gone, they both looked at him. "You didn't have to tell on us. You could have just asked us to not talk around you about it." He said that he'd told them several times not to talk about things they didn't know about. "We know a lot, Mr. Griffin. Or are we supposed to call you Lord of all the money, Griffin? Why are you here anyway?"

Putting little Jim in his bed, he turned to the nurses. He knew a great deal more about them than they thought they knew about him or the little boy's parents in this case. Thinking about what he was going to say, he simply smiled before he pulled out his notebook he'd been using since starting this project.

"I was going to write about the children that come in here. Their lives when they're born. How they're treated from hour one. But it's evolved into a book about how the nurses around here are just a few blowhards that thinks that just because they're behind a glass wall, which I've heard you mention as a way of gossiping for weeks, you're entitled to say whatever you want. But here are a few facts that you might now want to put out there. First of all, Beth, you should keep your mouth shut about being out of work. Has your husband worked a single day in his life since you got this job? No, he's not. And him saying he's a stay-at-home dad only works when there are children involved. You have none. Winny? When was the last time you saw your son? I heard that he's doing well now that he's with his grandparents. Having him taken from you because of your terrible drug habit is very telling. Last I heard, too, your husband will be getting out of prison soon and be home to knock you around a bit more before he either kills you or you kill him." He was told to keep his mouth shut. "Oh? Like the two of you do? Yes, I have money. And if you remember, when I was brought in here, I'm not getting any pay for this *volunteer* job. I was doing it for research, as you were both told. But a whole new storyline has come from it, and I'm thinking of calling it what nurses say about your baby when it's in their care. Do you think that would be a bestseller? I think so."

"You can't do that?" He asked her why not.

"Because people will know who you're talking about, and I won't have you talking about me when—"

"So it's all right for you to talk about other people, but the same can't be said about you. That's not very fair, is it?" He stood up to leave. As he was walking out the door, he told them to have a good life and that he was out of there.

He felt something touch him in the back of the head, more like a slam. When the same kind of pain took him to the floor for a second time, he tried to turn and fend off whatever was happening. The third blow knocked him out, and the last thing he remembered was that he was going to have a fucking hell of a headache when he woke up.

Waking up, startled by the light that was in his face, Harmon hurt his head more by moving away from it. There was a man in a white coat standing over him as well as a nurse that he could see behind him. While he wasn't able to make out faces, he could smell one of them was a wolf. Harmon was shocked when the doctor told him it was him.

"You talk out loud when you're out. Did you know that?" He said that he'd not but was glad to know. "All right, Mr. Griffin, my nurse here is going to give you some of the good stuff to help you with the headache that is more than likely making itself known to you about now. Then we're going to take you down for a C-scan to see what other damage might have been done to you."

By the time he returned to his room, his dad and older brother Edwin was there. He couldn't speak to them. He was nearly sick with the pain now. Almost as soon as he was in his bed again, Benji, the nurse that had been in the room before, was putting something in his IV. He felt it all the way to his toes.

When he woke a second time, his mom was there. The room was dark, and she warned him before turning on the overhead light. As soon as he could open his eyes against the glare, she hugged him gently and asked him why he'd not called her first.

"I didn't call anyone. I guess they looked at my employment record and called from there. I'm fine, Mom. You didn't have to come down here." She said he was her little boy. "I am, but I'm also a grown man that has been hurt before."

"I'm well aware of that, son." He smiled at her, and she smiled back. "Those nurses have been taken to the police station. I'm going to have a talk with their mothers too, see that I don't. I don't know all the things that you picked up on there, but it's been very helpful. Also, the camera's that Jeffery recently put in were very helpful as well. They have everything recorded. How are you really feeling?"

"Better now that I'm doped up a bit. Edwin told me when he was in here that they took my notebook. There are things in there that are going to get a lot of people in trouble, Mom. Is there any way that you can make sure that most of that stuff doesn't get out?" She asked him why she'd do that. "I don't want to get everyone fired."

"It's that bad?" He told her of a couple of things that he'd figured out. Mostly to do with the surgery and emergency departments. "They're stealing from them? What on earth would anyone need a sharps container for? Other than putting used needles in— never mind, I think I just answered my question. But the other things, tape and such, that can't be all that much, can it?"

"I figured it out a couple of weeks ago, and I believe it's about four cases a month of just gauze that is leaving here in lunch boxes. And don't get me started on the lunch room. There is a self-checkout part for employees that are on the second and third shifts that they're supposed to use. I doubt that one in fifteen are doing what they're supposed to be doing. Not to mention soda that they take out of here too." She sat down next to him and asked him what else he'd observed. "There are several affairs that are happening. In patient's rooms. Stuff that is not only unsanitary but also scary when you think about it."

"I'll have to get that notebook and do some house cleaning myself. No wonder the hospital is saying that they're not making as much profit as they had been. You'd think for as much money as we donate here, they'd be well-balanced and overflowing with things. This isn't right." He agreed with her and closed his eyes. The next thing he knew, he was waking up, and it was bright outside.

"Hello." He looked at Benji and asked her the time. "It's nearly noon now. When I came on shift this morning, I was told that you had a rough night. I've been making sure that you're resting well. Doctors orders. I also wanted to come by and thank you for what you did in the nursery. My sister is Winny."

"I'm so sorry about that." She told him not to worry about it and that Winny had always been a bitch. "I never said that, but since she hit me, I think she might be."

"She is. When I graduated from nursing

school, Winny found out how much I was making. I think she assumed that I didn't have to work all that hard for my money and decided that she'd be one too. After four tries of her boards, she works here too. Her and her friends, they never have anything to say about anyone that is good." He told her that he noticed that as well. "My mom, she wants to talk to you about her. Nothing bad, but she would like to hear your version of what happened in the hall other than just my sisters. Winny's making it sound as if you were hot to get her, and that justified her hurting you. If you had been human, you'd be dead by now, I guess."

"I would imagine so." They talked about this and that. Benji never seemed to be in a hurry to leave him. When she told him she had to go, it was nearly the end of her shift, and she thanked him again for his help. When he was alone, Harmon wondered what he was going to do for the rest of the night. Nothing he could think of off the top of his head. Which was beginning to hurt again.

"I'm glad to see that you've not shifted." Harmon must have fallen asleep again when he woke to hear a stranger's voice in his room. It was Doctor James again, the same one that had seen him in the emergency department. "I meant to tell you that before I left, not to heal yourself, but you seemed to have understood. The police will be by in the morning to talk to you about a few things that you had written down."

They talked about his injuries. He had a cracked skull as well as his shoulder had been dislocated. Apparently, the nurses had tried to drag him to the bathroom so that no one would find him. The elevator opening up had squashed those plans when several patients, as well as some of the staff, had caught them. He was glad that someone had found him before they tried to do him in.

"Your mom and dad have a meeting in the morning with the board. I haven't any idea what they're going to say, but I'd say that I've never seen your mom so upset before. She is going to take care of things she told me." Harmon told him he could count on her doing that if she had his notes. "I heard you were here to write a book. How many have you published so far?"

"Ten so far." Since he'd been around for nearly forever, he never told anyone the real number. He'd been writing some sort of book, children's, adult self helps, as well as romance, since he'd been a kid.

"Mostly, I just write things for the information that I find. I don't usually judge, but I think things got out of hand with this one."

"Yeah, I'd say you have that about right." They both laughed. "I heard good things about you working in the nursery, Harmon. I hope this doesn't keep you from coming in again and helping out. We need help with things like you were doing. Feeding and cleaning babies. Making sure that things are where they're supposed to be. Mable said that she enjoyed working with you while there."

"I enjoyed it myself. My brothers have children, and it's been helpful for me to be able to handle the little ones. Jeffery has four of the most adorable little girls. They melt my heart every time I see them." The doctor told him that he had three granddaughters and four grandsons. "My mom is busting at the seams. She's enjoying them all being around so much. I'm not ready for that just yet."

"Oh yeah? I thought that you and your unmarried brothers would be out looking for your mates. I know that I was when I was about your age. Of course, she didn't come along until later in my life, but that was all right as well. We have had a good life." He said nothing. While Harmon wasn't looking for a mate, he was looking forward to a life with one. And children. "Well, son, I'll let you get some rest. I just wanted to come by and make sure that you were pretty for the police when they showed up. You did us a good thing by reporting them. Indirectly, at least."

When he was alone again, he thought about himself having a mate. He did wonder at times if there was one out there for him, it wasn't like he was shy about meeting women, but he really didn't want to commit to anyone just yet. Harmon thought that his life was about the way he wanted it to be. He loved rules and women. At least the ones in his family didn't seem to understand those.

He lay there in the bed until his supper was brought to him. He was on a light diet as he'd had a head injury. Once he was finished with eating very little of the food, he decided that he wanted to get up in a chair for a while. Almost as soon as he was standing up, he regretted it.

The chair was nice, and he was comfortable sitting in it. However, he didn't look forward to making his way back to the bed. He was still dizzy and slightly ill to his belly, and the bright light from the sun setting was almost too much for his hurting head.

Once he was back in bed with more pain meds, he was trying to relax his body so that he could sleep off the pain. Before dozing off, he reached out to his family to tell them how much he loved them. Harmon had been hurt badly, and he decided that he didn't want to ever get to the point when he might be hurt so badly that he'd not be able to tell the ones that he loved how much he needed them in his life. He was going to do that more often too. Tell those that he loved that he was there for them as well.

AWARD WINNING, BESTSELLING AUTHOR

Kathi Barton, a winner of the Pinnacle Book Achievement Award and a best-selling author on Amazon and All Romance books, lives in Nashport, Ohio, with her husband, Paul. When not creating new worlds and romance, Kathi and her husband enjoy camping and going to auctions. She can also be seen at county fairs with her husband, an artist and potter.

Her muse, a cross between Jimmy Stewart and Hugh Jackman, brings her stories to life for her readers in a way that has them returning for more. Her favorite genre is paranormal romance, with a great deal of spice. You can visit Kathi online and email her if you'd like. She loves hearing from her fans. aaronskiss@gmail.com